What Others Are Saying

I feel blessed to know Susan Brunner as an author, radio personality, and woman of faith. She is authentic in her writing and her daily walk. Susan is a regular guest on my radio program, *Senior Agenda with Lisa Stockdale*, as one of our "Sassy Seniors." We never know if Susan is going to leave us giggling or pondering some deep truth delivered as only she can deliver. These same observations are mirrored in her written work. She is naturally engaging. She writes, speaks, and lives from the heart.

—Lisa Stockdale
Radio Personality & Host, Senior
Agenda with Lisa Stockdale
www.talktainmentradio.com

Tit-for-Tat

Tit-for-Tat

Tit-for-Tat

SUSAN KAY BOX BRUNNER

Published by FWB Publications, Columbus, Ohio 43207

Published in the United States of America
ISBN: 978-1-940609-75-1
Fiction / General
14.12.09

Acknowledgments

I wish to acknowledge the following people for their services: Gail Tipton-Castle and Chris Tucker, my photographers; Christie Burke-Crawford, my encourager with a listening ear; Mandy Larger, who spent many hours editing for typos and grammatical errors; and Beth Loughner, for her direction in the March of Life (MOL) trilogy.

—Chickadee, Melissa Tucker,
Thank you for your time and words of wisdom!

1

Mariah News entered the ground floor elevator of the NYC's Hotel and impatiently tapped her long red nail on the elevator button. While looking down her nose, she waited for the bell to ding for the fifty-third floor. As the door opened at her floor, her jaw dropped. She mouthed, "What the—" at seeing the bright yellow caution tape stretched across her penthouse suite's doorway.

Catching her breath, Mariah screeched, "I purchased a high-riser suite. Why?" She proceeded in her nine-inch heels, ducked under the caution tape, and clicked her way into her suite.

Mariah flinched to an eerie sound, and it caused her to turn. She watched in disbelief as her newly installed cypress door dropped from its dangled position onto the floor. Mariah's knees weakened. She stepped backwards, and her arms reached out for the makeshift kitchen counter. Mariah breathed out, "Now would be a great time for Karen's sweet mint chocolate brewed iced tea."

Blowing out a held breath, she willed calmness. Rolling her hazel eyes, Mariah saw all the unfinished work of her suite. Suddenly, the hairs on her neck bristled and her heart raced; she wasn't alone. Clearing her throat, she turned slowly, and in front of her stood a man she had met while staying at her brother's farm. Her breath caught; he was so handsome. He appeared taller and tanner, and he was shirtless. Mariah lifted her shaky index finger and squealed, "What are you doing in my suite, Joshua Jimso Brown?"

J. J. cocked his head and his boyish grin faded. He replied, "Call me J. J. And I believe a thank-you would be nice, for I'm working. Your brother asked me to keep an eye out for you." The corners of his mouth lifted again, and the smile carried through his shy blue eyes.

"Get out!" she yelled, stomping her foot. Just seeing him again made her insides shake. What was it about that man!

J. J. placed a hand on his bare chest. "Woman, for an educated person, you're a spoiled brat." He walked toward the front door, muttering, "Just because she's a world traveler and her grandparents are royalty." J. J. knelt and touched the recently laid imported marble floor.

Mariah shrieked, "Now what are you doing?"

J. J. pulled a notepad from his back pocket and replied, "Observing." Tucking the pad away, he grabbed his shirt and pushed his muscular arms through the sleeves. He walked a short distance, bent down, and began working on the cherry wood kitchenette set.

Mariah's pale-ivory face heated to a brilliant beet red. In a strained voice, she growled, "You have some nerve, mister, being in my suite, uninvited." She fanned herself.

Just then the phone rang. Mariah hesitated in answering and shouted, "Get out J. J.!" Letting out another breath, she blurted into the phone's receiver, "Hello, Mariah News speaking."

"Hi, sis! This is Ken, your brother." Chuckling, he said, "Need I ask how your day is going?"

Mariah hit the speaker button, freeing both hands. She was still pointing at J. J. She roared, "I know who this is, brother dear." Then, in a frantic voice, she asked, "Is Miechael all right?"

Ken answered, "We're all fine."

"So why the call?"

In his acquired southern drawl, he said, "I've making sure you're safe in New York. Mariah, by the way, have you seen J. J.?" The line crackled, but she heard him say, "I asked him to keep an eye out for you in the big city."

"Ken, I've traveled the world over, studied abroad, and have lived on my own." She clicked her tongue. "First, I'm doing just fine in New York." Lowering her voice, she said, "I wished you hadn't encouraged that man, J. J." She stretched the cord and bunched her lips, noticing J. J. was wearing that silly smile; his ocean blue eyes were captivating.

"Are you still there, sis?" The static stopped, and he added, "I do have another reason for my call and a rather serious request."

Mariah tapped her heel, spurting out, "I'm here. What do you want?"

Slowly, in almost a whisper, Ken asked, "Could Miechael stay awhile longer with us in Mississippi? The boys and Sara and I would like more time with him."

Mariah blinked her flecking hazel eyes. "I'm not sure Miechael should." Her voice softened. "I miss him so."

Ken blurted out, "What's with the noise?"

Mariah irritatingly answered, "Its J. J. using a hammer."

"So he's there. Great." Ken cleared his throat. "Sis, I'm sure you're missing your son. He misses you too. However, the yearly Leakesville's outdoor drama theatric presentation opens Friday night. Then the following Thursday, our community's Cotton Fair opens. If Miechael could stay, he could have a better understanding of American culture and learn more of his Southern family's roots." Ken hesitated. "However, the decision is yours, Mariah." Silence. Ken quickly added, "Our fair is featuring historic antique farm equipment versus today's modern equipment. Some local farmers and corporate businessmen are giving speeches, and they will illustrate the use of the old and new equipment. Ah, come on, Mariah, all the children look forward to these events and all the 4H farm animals."

Mariah managed to say, "Well."

Ken chuckled a little. "I like the sheep shearing myself. It's quite a sight. The shearers enter a contest, each trying to outdo the other on who shears their sheep the fastest. Oh, I wish you could be here, Mariah."

"I can't. I have modeling interviews, a career to seek."

"I know. And I understand the importance of this modeling career, striking out on your own path." Ken let out a held breath. "Mariah, our fair is also filled with fun. It has a Ferris wheel, a merry-go-round, and even pony rides." He waited.

Mariah's eyes darted around the room, and tears formed. She blurted out, "Ken my penthouse suite is nowhere near completion. The cabinets aren't stained or even hung, and there isn't any flooring in the bathroom. As a matter of fact, I'm looking at box after box of unused tiles. And there are five-gallon paint cans, unopened." She clicked her tongue and swatted at her eyes. "Ken, the hotel management has squeezed me into the smallest apartment quarters I've ever seen, under the umbrella, complements of the hotel. My suite is so in disarray." She sniffed. Finally she said, "All right Ken, Miechael may stay for just a little while longer."

Ken calmly replied, "Thank you, sis. Call whenever you want. I know your decision is heartfelt. But Mariah, know that I love you."

Still sniffling, Mariah waved a hand and willed composure.

"Sis?"

She replied, "We'll talk soon. Please mention to Miechael to call me. Good-bye."

J. J. stood with his hands on his narrow hips. "Such a nice thing for you to allow your son to visit longer with his uncle. Ken's a nice man."

Mariah clenched and unclenched her hand and glared at him with her hazel eyes. Through gritted teeth, she uttered, "I told you to leave! I don't need your or anyone else's opinion on what's best for my son. I've taken care of us since I first found out I was pregnant."

J. J. threw his hands over his head and walked from the suite. She placed a call to maintenance. Slamming down the receiver, she looked up and jumped. A burly man sporting a badge stood in the exposed doorway. She gasped and quickly began lecturing him. "How dare you leave my suite unprotected? Do you know who I am?"

More security personnel arrived. They jumped through hoops as she barked out orders. Suddenly J. J. reappeared, carrying a tool kit and whistling. He walked directly past her to the table and began hammering. Without a word, he finally set the table upright and placed four chairs around it.

Mariah grabbed the security man's arm, yelling, "Get him out of here!" Mariah watched closely with folded arms.

J. J. brushed his hands against his tight-fitting jeans then removed his earplugs. She bit her lower lip when his sea blue eyes met hers and lingered. J. J. broke contact and walked toward the security guard, calling him by name. They continued walking from the suite. Mariah hustled after them, calling out, "Wait, wait, Mr. Security, you don't understand."

J. J. rushed back and hoisted Mariah under his arm like a sack of potatoes. He stepped back inside her suite, saying, "We need to talk." He thought, *If only Mariah would listen. She needs to know that he pleaded with Eurlene to get the hotel's manager and Mr. Afee to accommodate her with their services.*

"Put me down." She jerked, wiggling her feet and hands. "Now!"

He obeyed, thinking, *She's a hot mess.*

Mariah reached into a box and threw books at him. "You big ox!"

J. J. dodged right then left as the books sailed past him. He glanced from under his arm. Seeing the box was now empty, his eyes locked with Mariah's.

Moisture formed around her gold-flecked hazel eyes.

Jamming his hands in his pockets, he asked, "What's wrong?"

The phone rang again. Mariah sniffled, but she answered, "Hello, Mariah News." She blew out a breath, raised a brow, and caught J. J.'s eye. She covered the phone, saying, "There's an unidentified woman on the other end of my line demanding she talk with Joshua Brown." Clearing her throat, she spoke more calmly into the receiver, "Please wait." She rolled her darkened hazel eyes and all but threw him the phone. "Joshua Brown, take this."

His eyebrows lifted. "There's a call for me?"

Mariah made a fist.

"This is J. J. What?"

Mariah watched in disbelief at his easiness.

Chuckling, he asked, "Now? Okay, give me thirty minutes." J. J. handed Mariah the phone and said, "Thank you. See you later." Stooping, he picked up the toolbox and swaggered from the suite.

Mariah flopped on a kitchenette chair, clenching and unclenching her hands and thinking, *What is it about that man? He's so—irritating! And I don't want to have emotional feelings for another man.* Suddenly the antique gold ivory clock on the unstained mantel sounded. All thoughts of J. J. were pushed aside. She needed to hurry, and she had no choice but to use the suite's unfinished bathroom and change into her modeling wardrobe. She applied theatrical makeup and smoothed her flowing, silky, raven hair, clasping it to the side. Grabbing her London Fog coat, Mariah left the unguarded penthouse suite. She pushed the elevator button and reached ground level.

From the hotel, she didn't flag down a cab or stop by her favorite coffee shop. Instead, she hurriedly walked to Murray and W. Broadway Street to meet up with her agent. She licked her red, red lips while waiting, remembering what her agent had said, "This modeling gig is a soap commercial to be featured on national television. And it offers a three-year contract." He had added, "They only need one model."

Mariah searched up and down the streets, but still there wasn't any agent. She straightened and marched into the huge building and walked over to the receptionist desk. She smugly smiled and signed in. Mariah sat perfectly upright, waiting for her name to be called.

She watched as female after female model left with sad expressions. They seemed defeated, some with slumped shoulders and others leaving in a fury.

Mariah caught a glimpse of her agent rounding the corner with an apparent television personnel and a cameraman. She stood up and without waiting for introductions, she slipped off the London Fog coat and posed. The cameraman's beady eyes lifted. The TV personnel jabbed the cameraman, and the snapping began. Mariah modeled with ownership. She made eye contact with her agent and winked. Miles's jaw dropped.

He leaned in, saying, "Brilliant, Mariah."

The television personnel said, "You're an exotic sort."

Miles nudged him, smiling. "She is."

The personnel continued. "Intoxicating, she has a most unusual look. Very photographic, and those huge smoky hazel eyes of hers scream danger." He turned his wedding band and, never breaking eye contact with Mariah, said to Miles, "I wonder if her skin is as soft and velvety as it appears."

Her full, shiny red lips pouted. She struck another pose knowingly. The fluffy black feathers on her spiked slip-on slippers enhanced her legs.

When the photo shoot ended, Miles, the TV personnel, and Mariah walked into his office. The producer motioned to them both to sit. He said, "Mariah, you're breathtaking and quite mystifying in that little number. You're beyond striking."

Miles pinched his mouth and opened his briefcase. He nodded in agreement with all the financial arrangements. The producer left the room. Miles's leaned in to Mariah, held out her London Fog coat, and said, "Put this on, sign on the dotted line, step outside this office, and wait for me."

She huffed, grabbed her coat, signed the papers, and left the room.

Miles joined Mariah shortly and clutched her elbow, saying, "Dinner is on me." He presented her with two additional modeling contracts. The producer's brother owned a cosmetic company, which would be featuring a new lineup of red lipsticks. And his sister owned a business selling imported women's hats and accessories.

Mariah looked over the contracts and the sizeable amount offered to her. She giggled and reached for Miles's pen and quickly signed her name without batting an eyelash. Mariah said, "Miles, darling, thanks for dinner. Ciao!" She stood up gracefully and winked at a young male cashier as she passed by. She suppressed a snicker as the men in the restaurant watched. She noticed that the women even paused and stared until she disappeared.

Mariah, back in her hotel room, placed a call to her grandparents. On the first ring, she said, "Hello, Grandmother."

"Mariah, it's wonderful to hear from you. Is everything all right, dear? Do you need money?"

"No, Grandmother. I'm so excited. I've signed three modeling contracts today, and payday begins in two weeks. Grandmother, I still have money left from the money you and grandfather wired me last month." Mariah cleared her throat, and on impulse, she added, "My suite is terrible!"

"What's wrong?"

"The contractor works at a snail's pace."

"Mariah," her grandmother said, "did you remember to have the contractor sign a contract? You know Grandfather would surely speak with him."

"Yes, Grandmother, but no to Grandfather's call."

Her grandmother snapped, "He'll not put up with laziness."

Mariah sighed. "Grandmother, both of us agreed upon the work, stipulating that he has up to six months to complete the job. It's entirely my fault."

"Grandfather can call him."

"No, Grandmother, I'm meeting up with the contractor tonight at 6:00 pm. I'll offer more money, and hopefully he'll work daily on my suite."

Grandmother paused then asked, "How's Miechael adjusting in New York?"

"He's fine."

"May I have a word with him?"

Mariah cleared her throat, and then she said, "Miechael is not with me. He's living with Ken and his family while my penthouse suite is under construction."

"Oh? Mr. News lives on a farm! All those stinky cows and horse animals."

"Grandmother, stop. Ken's a good man." Mariah counted slowly then softly added, "Thank you though for all your help, and tell Grandfather I said hello. But bye for now."

Another three long months passed. Mariah woke up with a cramped neck. Looking around, she said, "I'm so tired of this cramp space of accommodation the hotel management has provided. If only my plush suite was done." She stretched and added, "The only advantage of staying here at the hotel is in using its name." Mariah glanced at the small lumpy bed and walked from the room, stating, "I'm glad Miechael is at my brother's farm. Ken's lifestyle with his wife and two boys is healthy and stable. What a fortunate man." Dressing, she nervously laughed and said, "It's hard to believe Ken is a successful CPO of a Mississippi bank. He's so patient and relaxed. And at home, he's a real natural in his jeans and cowboy boots." She thought, *Ken is a rather good-*

looking man when he's riding a horse or mucking out stalls—a cowboy through and through.

Riding to the top floor, she complained, "Elevators take way too long, and I need to inform the manager." The elevator door opened. She gasped. Unscheduled hammering and loud buzzing noises roared from her suite. It was music to her ears, but when she stepped inside, there stood rugged J. J. Her breath caught, and her stomach rolled. His back was to her, and she secretly admired him, his muscles and their movement. She let out a held breath. He was shirtless again. Her eyes trailed from his broad shoulders to where his jeans rested on his narrow hips. Her heart raced faster. She noticed there wasn't a hint of a color difference. She felt hot.

"Hello, Mariah, see anything you like? Or are you going to stand there like a bump on a log?" He ran a hand through his cropped red hair, and crinkles formed around his sea blue eyes.

Her heart plumped to her stomach. She reddened and shouted, "Stop this! Why wasn't I called?"

Her contractor appeared from the kitchen, reached for her arm, and gingerly guided Mariah into another room. He shouted orders over his shoulder. "Men, continue working." His jaw was set in a fine line.

Maria jerked her arm away and glanced back at J. J. She bit her lip and wondered, *Why is he here?*

The contractor's eyes narrowed.

Mariah stopped her walk and pointed a finger at him. "Why wasn't I called before the work was under way?"

The contractor inhaled and with his hand on hip said, "I can quit, Miss News. I'm not on your schedule, remember? However, my men are on mine. You did approve of the new work contract." His eyes shifted, and then in a calmer manner, he stated, "Ma'am, I only want your suite to sing praises of my work and of your trusted taste."

"Well, Mr. Afee, what if I want any changes?"

"Fair enough." He kept a keen eye contact. "Understand, Miss News, the work is just roughed in. Try trusting me." He plastered a smiled and added, "Why don't you leave your suite and, let's say, come back later at, say, 1:15 p.m. We'll do a walk-through, and I'll take notes should there be any changes."

Mariah wasn't used to being dismissed.

"All right, Miss News?"

"I'll be back!" She turned, wanting to face J. J. and give him a piece of her mind. But she found no trace of him. She sighed. "He's good at disappearing." In her nine-inch heels, she marched from the suite. The hotel manager flagged her.

"Miss News, there you are. I'm glad I've caught you. There's a gentleman waiting on the downstairs main phone line named Mr. Day."

She made many quick short steps and hurried from the elevator. On the house phone, she said, "Hello, this is Mariah News."

"Hello, this is Jud Day, your brother's friend and coworker. Do you remember us meeting?"

"Yes." And she silently thought, *Nice, muscular-built older man with the greenest of eyes and oozing with charm!* Clearing her throat, she said, "We met briefly at Ken's farmhouse a few months ago. What's up?"

"Well, Miss News, my wife, Karen, heard you would like some of her specialty brewed tea. As I am scheduled in New York for a banker's conference, I could arrange to stop by the hotel and give you a quart of the mint chocolate green tea."

Mariah said, "However did Karen know I've been dying to try her tea?"

Jud chuckled, "Women. Sara and her mother, Louise, placed a two-way call to Karen, and your name came up. Sara mentioned you were interested in her specialty brew tea. And the rest is history."

Mariah gasped, "Thank you, Mr. Day. It would be very nice of you to drop by. Shall we meet in the lobby? And do thank Karen, or Mrs. Day, for me. When shall I expect you?"

Jud replied, "My plane lands in New York Friday. Say, 2:00 p.m."

She opened her mouth to answer, but the line was dead. On Friday, Mariah met with Jud, secretly admiring his great looks and manners; they were exceptional especially for an older man in his late thirties. Communication flowed as with her brother, Ken. Mariah thanked him for the brewed tea Karen sent.

Jud's mouth turn up at the corners when he said, "Karen offered you, Ms. News, an open invitation to stay at the bed-and-breakfast. Perhaps your modeling work will bring you our way."

Mariah tapped her long slender fingers on the table. She grabbed her newly acquired purse from Sara and reached for her appointment book. Straightening, she observed Jud sitting with his leg across his other knee. She glanced upward, and she saw that his jawline showed traces of the five-o'clock shadow. He seemed truly happy. His right dimple deepened. She quickly but mentally noted to herself, *Karen must know how Jud affects women.*

She cleared her throat. "I'll call Karen direct. I do need to be in Ohio the last part of August." She scrunched her nose. "It would be nice to holiday there while working."

Jud replied, "Just call." He slipped Mariah Karen's business card. Adjusting his silk tie, he sipped coffee and then glanced in Mariah's direction. "Say, have you seen J. J. since you've arrived?"

Mariah's face dropped. "What?" She blew out a held breath.

"Oh, that Joshua Brown. He's a sad, sad excuse for a human being. I've seen him all right. He just lives three and a half minutes from me." Laughing, Jud waved his hands.

Mariah inhaled a breath. "He butts into my business all the time. He knows the architect and is quite the artist at disappearing when I want to see him."

"Whoa," Jud said. "I just thought it would be nice to know someone your own age, living in the big city, but my goodness." He gave another chuckle before looking at his watch. Jud stood up. "I have a meeting within the hour so I better head to the bank."

She stood up, shook his hand, and again thanked him for the tea. Mariah waited until Jud left the building before climbing the stairs. She saw J. J. enter the elevator. She fumed. But she was surprised when she saw a fresh bouquet of roses sitting on her kitchenette table. She read the card.

> Hi beautiful, be ready by seven. I have tickets for the opera. *Porgy and Bess* are playing. We'll have a late dinner. Sorry about last-minute plans, but the Artist House just called with available tickets.
>
> J. J.

"What?" She muttered. "Attend with him?" Then she reasoned out, "He is highly ranked on the social ladder. Besides"—she twirled around—"it would look good, and being seen with him could only get me noticed more." She nodded. "It's a public place. It's safe. Why not?"

2

If only I hadn't promised Ken to help out his sister out in New York, J. J. thought. J. J. had changed his work schedule so as not to run daily into Mariah. He said, "I must be nuts to work so hard for free. And wow, what a temper she has." He smiled. "However, she is a rare creature, and what a beauty!" At times he had to escape and breathe deeply or he would expose his feelings to Mariah. "Her attitude though is a royal pain in the a——." He thought, *My sister comes across as a snob, but Mariah is one!* He sat in an overstuffed chair, babbling, "I don't know how such a down-to-earth person like Ken News could have a sister like Mariah."

J. J. opened his mail, and realization hit. He hadn't dated anyone since his return to New York, nor had he returned any female's calls. "Why have I shied away from public engagements?" He rubbed his chin and sighed. "The limelight just doesn't hold the meaning it once did."

It was late, and J. J. was restless. For some reason, while in the shower, Mariah's face flashed before him. His stomach knotted, and sweat broke on his brow. As the cool water cascaded down his back, he said, "It isn't like I haven't been around the block a time or two. What's so different about Mariah?" He shook his wet red hair and said, "It's always me who brushes off the ladies."

He slipped between the sheets and found another sleepless night. J. J. grabbed his robe and made a vow, "I'll date Mariah. I'll wine, dine, and show her a good time. And I'll be a real gentleman. And surely Mariah's enchanting hold on me will wear off." His mind trailed. *Growing up, his sister had warned him about certain women.* He said, "She'll beg me for a kiss, and I will oblige."

Looking into the mirror, his nostrils flared. "I can walk away from her anytime." He felt his head, thinking he must have a touch of flu coming on. He sat on his 1900 Posturepedic bed and glanced out the ceiling-to-floor window. He raked his hair, saying, "I only have interest in her because she's so mysterious." He exhaled, realizing he wanted more than friendship with Mariah. "Ken will kill me."

A few evenings later, J. J. admired himself in the mirror and smugly said, "You handsome devil." He winked and adjusted his bow tie. "What doesn't a man do to woo a woman's company— especially one like Mariah?" He thought about all the called-in favors; he had rented a limousine and reserved a table at the famous Riese Restaurant. He patted his tuxedo pocket once again, making sure he had the opera tickets. J. J. slid on his white gloves and then put on his top hat. Just then room service knocked at his apartment door and handed him the special flowers he had ordered for Mariah. He smiled at his matching boutonniere.

He stepped into the shared elevator. Women gawked, and some batted their eyes at him. It was the same when he entered the lobby of the hotel. Someone even stepped in front and snapped a picture. He blinked, seeing spots. Another man clapped him on the back and asked, "Who's the lucky woman tonight?"

Despite his excitement, he just waved and kept on walking. He signaled to the limo driver. When he entered the limo, he was pleased at seeing the stocked bar. His ride ended in three and half minutes; they had arrived at Mariah's residence. The driver waited, and photos were snapped again. He paused as the elevator dinged. He watched as Mariah stepped into the hotel foyer. The photographers suddenly shifted from him to her. He let out a low whistle admiring Mariah slowly from head to toe and back meeting her eyes. Her hair was gathered in an upswept do. Her gown was an electrifying blue and draped to the floor. It hugged every curve and revealed her leg from the right side. He gasped.

Every man looked on. A weakness hit his chest; Mariah was definitely a breathtaking vision. He dusted off his flawless sleeve and moved closer to his date. He whispered, "Darling, you are exquisite." Her fragrance floated through the air, bringing scents of light citrus and sweet honeysuckle flowers. His legs threatened to buckle.

Mariah took a step backwards. "Thanks, Mr. Brown. And for the lovely flowers, left in my suite." Noticing that he held an orchid corsage, she asked, "For me?"

He stiffened, but he steeled himself, smiled, and reached for her arm. He struggled to speak, and his anger surged. He guided her to the limo where the driver stood at attention.

She tapped her foot, and the driver clicked his feet together, bowing.

J. J. sat across from her. He wasn't surprised when she waved out the window.

The limo pulled to the curb in front of the opera house. She watched J. J. as men flashed tickets to sell. Mariah momentarily touched his hand, saying, "I know for a fact that the opera house tickets have been sold out for months."

Nodding, he said not a word but only stood wearing his known crooked smile. He squeezed her hand, urging her toward the door.

They were approached for pictures. They stopped and posed for the public and for the photographers.

One man said, "Mr. Brown, You're looking demure. And who's the, um, lady?"

He gave no answer. But J. J. whispered in her hearing, "Aren't you glad you came with me?"

Mariah jabbed his ribs and slapped his chin in her excitement. He stepped back with his hurt jaw, holding his cheek. A bright flash appeared. J. J. rubbed his eyes.

She glanced in his direction and said, "You surprised me by really having tickets."

He only smiled. Both Mariah and J. J. climbed the stairs and found their seats. She reached and pulled the binoculars from around J. J.'s neck, pointing to the stage. "I need to see the singers in costumes as they step from the rising curtain."

J. J. coughed and turned in his seat, gawking at Mariah.

She said, "The balcony view is excellent."

J. J. nodded. "The acoustics in here make everything sound as if it's in surround sound." His stomach tightened when she touched his arm. He realized Mariah made him feel different. He thought, *She isn't like any woman I've ever met or dated*. His hands trembled.

During intermission, Mariah said, "J. J., a cup of imported tea would be nice."

Excusing himself, he waited in a long line for their beverage.

He watched as Mariah tilted the cup and touched it with her luscious full lips.

In disbelief, she shivered and made a horrible face. Mariah squared her shoulders, lifted her head a little too high, but gracefully said, "Please excuse me."

He nodded and stood in the foyer, waiting. Minutes passed. The flickering lights warned people to be seated. He tapped his foot impatiently; still no Mariah. The light dimmed the second time. There was clapping, and the second half of the program began. J. J. was alarmed. He found a cleaning staff member and asked her to check out the ladies' room for Mariah.

Within moments, she returned. "Sir, there is no one inside the ladies area. Sorry." She scurried away.

Mystified, he looked around and became wide-eyed when he saw Mariah waving down from the balcony. He mumbled,

"What's wrong with her? She isn't making this date easy. I should have stayed at home." He fisted his hands, but he forced a smile and proceeded in the dark to his seat. He settled in as the singers preformed another number. Only his attention was on Mariah, and he drank in her loveliness as she watched the opera. All too soon, the houselights came up. The people stood up and cheered, "Bravo! Bravo!"

She handed him the binoculars and slithered past him down the steps. He followed then reached for her arm, keeping his eyes lowered. The chauffeur bent, tipped his hat, and quietly opened the door for her and J. J. The limousine ride was tense. The driver parked outside the restaurant.

Mariah touched J. J.'s arm and asked, "Would you mind Chinese takeout instead?"

He frowned. "What?" Then a bubble of laughter escaped from his lips. "Yes, we can get takeout. Drive on William."

The limousine moved in and out of traffic and arrived at Mariah's hotel. He walked Mariah to the door of her temporary dwelling place and waited while she slipped the key in the door. Once inside, Mariah quickly turned and held out her hand to J. J. and asked, "Where's my food container?" She leaned in, kissed his cheek, batted her hazel eyes, and said, "Thank you for the night out at the opera. I am sorry you weren't able to fine a real date being the last minute and all. But I had wanted to see *Porgy and Bess*, so thanks for asking me." As she closed the door, she said, "I have an early photo shoot in the morning, you understand." Then she locked the door.

Confused, J. J. walked to the limo, paid the bill, tipped the driver, and sprinted to his flat carrying his container of food. Standing once more in a cold, cold cascading shower, he felt mortified. He blurted out, "She's good." J. J. threw the container of food out and padded to the bed to have another sleepless night.

The phone rang. J. J. grabbed a pillow and covered his head. The ringing continued. He opened one eye and grumbled. "It's dark outside. Who would be calling this early? It isn't even the crack of dawn." J. J. sat up and barked into the phone, "Hello, speak up before I slam this receiver down."

"J. J., what's your problem?"

J. J. blinked. His blue eyes narrowed. He was now wide-awake. "Sis? Eurlene, what's wrong?"

Eurlene screeched, "Have you seen this morning's newspaper?"

"No! You just got me out of bed. Wait." Rushing to the door, he stooped and reached for the newspaper. His mouth dropped. There on the front page was the picture of Mariah slapping him. The article read, "Socialite Joshua 'Jimso' Brown insulted Miss Mariah News, royalty of the Duke and Lady Harold Ma Mere. His immaturity is on a downward spiral. How will this be explained?"

Holding his head, he said, "What the——?" Picking up the receiver, he said, "I see. Yes, I read it. Let me explain. It isn't as it seems. Mariah's hit to my chin was just a fun jester. She wasn't angry with me." Under his breath, he stated, "Not at the moment. Honestly, Eurlene, she was only pleasantly surprised with the opera tickets.. I'm sorry about the photo, but this time I didn't do anything wrong, Eurlene."

Sternly and unwavering he heard in Eurlene's raspy voice, "J. J. I've booked you on a flight to Ohio, Jud's place. You're staying at the bed-and-breakfast that his wife, Karen, runs. Be on the 5:10 a.m. flight. The plane leaves in forty-five minutes. And Jud's expecting you."

"Eurlene?" The line went silent.

Jud was in New York and had rushed to a meeting with his attorney, Spencer, and Eurlene, who was the president of Upper New York's bank. Jud arrived two hours late because of the heavy traffic. When he entered the bank, their host handed him a sealed envelope addressed to him from Spencer. The letter read,

Jud, we are experiencing great difficulties from a legal standpoint. I had to fly suddenly to Rome. Eurlene is presently with me. Please be notified of my deepest regret in the postponement of our meeting. It needs to be rescheduled at your end. Also include Ken and Joshua perhaps at your establishment in Columbus, Ohio. Let's set the time for the month of August.

He looked at his watch, and a long sigh escaped. "Oh, New York's traffic!" He glanced at his return ticket and saw that he only had a two-hour wait. He buttoned up his topcoat, raised his arm, and hailed a cab. He muttered, "People are always in a hurry." And then someone stepped in front of him and whizzed into the cab.

He shoved Spencer's notice inside the envelope and noticed a small scrap of paper caught on it. He pulled out the short paper and found a handwritten note from Eurlene.

Dearest Jud, J. J. has gotten bad press coverage again. Please rescue me. Allow him to be your aid in your bank in Ohio. He really is a great little brother, but his decisions sometimes aren't thought out beforehand. I've included the newspaper article. Jud, I know your influence on him is highly valued. Taken God's into account. I will always be endeared to you.

At the airport, he babbled, "How can I answer her? Eurlene's gone." Rubbing his chin and chuckling, he said, "After all this time, Eurlene still has faith in me. Hmm, she sure knows how to get her way."

The flight was short, and hailing a cab to his house was easy. Stepping into the kitchen, he set down his luggage and viewed Karen. He smiled. She possessed a quiet beauty in her own right. She had tossed her blond hair into a ponytail, and a few tendrils were dangling around her sweetheart face. His attention was drawn from her and the pot she was stirring when the phone rang. Karen gracefully turned the fire on low.

She answered on the second ring. "KD Bed-and-Breakfast."

Just then the twins, Luke and Luci, let out huge screams.

"Not me!"

"Yes you."

"No, no, no, you."

Karen turned, looking forlorn. She waved and motioned Jud toward the children. Saluting, he marched to the sounds coming from the basement, where he observed Jack standing beside both children and pointing a finger. Luci saw her dad and poked Luke. Both ran to him. One grabbed one leg, and the other twin wrapped their arms around his waist. Jud said, "What a wet mess and yet what trust!" He smiled then waved to Jack. He stooped and listened as both twins pleaded their case. He whisked them upstairs, one under each arm. He turned on the shower. "Luke showers first." Then he motioned to Luci and said, "Afterward, you twins join me in the bedroom."

They entered with their heads hung. Jud said, "Each of you need to pray."

Luci, prim and proper, began. "You should know that he pulled my hair, and that's a sin."

Luke reached his hand over to her with eyes wide open. He squealed, "I told you I was sorry."

Keeping her eyes closed, Luci continued. "He was rude to me."

Jud, with narrowed eyes, heard her appeal, and he saw Luke's sincerity. Luci stopped praying and began to cry. Luke glanced at his father and pulled on his hand. "Help, Dad."

Jud gave a sigh and patted both children on their shoulders. Luci lunged forward and hugged her twin brother. At the same time, both said, "I'm sorry."

Jud shook his head for he really didn't know what their issues had been, but he was glad it appeared over. Now maybe he could seek out his wife.

Karen stood on the edge of the stairway and straightened her apron. She announced, "Dinner."

Jud caught the tenderness in her sky blue eyes as she spoke with the children and then glanced up at him. Her beauty still affected him. He grabbed the guardrail as he walked toward her. Her lips turned upward as he placed an arm around her waist. Leaning in and squeezing, he whispered, "May I bed you tonight?"

3

There was back-to-back phone ringing, the doorbell chimed, and there still sat Jud's luggage. Karen said, "Twins, march to the kitchen, retrieve another place setting, and set the table." Karen reached for the phone, and Jud answered the front door.

"Hello, J. J."

With his coat in hand, J. J. set down his luggage and extended his right hand. "Sir, my sister, Eurlene, asked me to fly here and assist you at your bank."

Jud choked. "Hmm." A smile reached his eyes. "I believe a better word would be, *ordered*." Jud placed an arm around J. J. "Come on in and let's eat."

J. J. paled as he entered the dining area. He glanced toward Karen and said, "Hello, and surprise."

Jud winked at Karen, knowing she always set an extra place. He signaled J. J. to the designated seat. Karen hung up the phone and quietly came to the table. The rest of the evening was routine. However, at around midnight, Jud heard a loud knock at the kitchen door. Rubbing his eyes, he nudged Karen, picked up a baseball bat, and ambled down the stairs.

"Well, hello, Claudia!"

Laughing, she slapped Jud on the shoulder and said, "My plane got in sooner than I expected. I thought the flight was p.m., but it was early a.m. Well, here I am anyway. Its okay, ain't it?"

Jud smiled and took her worn coat and her battered suitcase.

Karen, in a terry robe, appeared in the kitchen by candlelight. Giggling, she told Jud to carry Claudia's suitcase to room 3C.

"Claudia," Karen said after a hug, "it's good to see you. Are you hungry?"

"Sure, a little."

"Come, I'll brew us some hot tea. Would you like some pastries or a sandwich? Peach cobbler or cherry?"

Stroking her chin, Claudia said, "Hot peach cobbler, thank you. Then she added, "Jack is to be here tomorrow for dinner. Did that horse's tail let you know he was coming? Did Jack make all the necessary arrangements? He said, 'This is the proper place for us to meet and discuss our future plans."

Jud's eyes widened as Karen muffled a laugh. "I knew he was coming, but not when, but tomorrow night is fine. Mariah will be here. You know she's Ken's sister, and she has agreed to chaperone. I talked with her earlier and confirmed her flight. Claudia, Mariah also has a modeling event right here at our local hat shop."

Karen passed Claudia a lit candle for her use in her room. Pausing in the doorway, Karen said, "Breakfast is at seven a.m. sharp. I trust you will have a fine rest."

Jud reached the bed first and was resting on one arm. His eyes brightened, and he smiled when Karen stepped from the bathroom. He patted the bed for her to join him. Without delay, she blew out the candle and slid under the sheet. Her feminine scent drifted under his nose as he bent to brush her lips. He could still taste the cherry dessert. Her fingers slid from the nape of his neck. She tugged his hair. He breathed out, "Karen?"

Karen bucked a little and blushed. She tilted and whispered, "I see promise and also a glint of wickedness in your bright emerald eyes."

Karen and Jud laughed, and arm in arm, they headed to the kitchen.

Breakfast awaited on the warming table. There was a display of pancakes, a plate of sunny-side up eggs, sausages, and bacon.

The morning drinks included coffee, orange juice, water, and a choice of hot or iced tea. They were all for self-service.

The twins slept in. Conversation flowed with Jud, Karen, Claudia, and Mariah as they sat around the large table. J .J. bounced in, and his jaw dropped. His eyes squinted; he found he was sitting next to Mariah. He said, "Mariah, what are you doing here?"

Mariah's sharp smile was plastered to her face. "Hello, Mr. Brown." She snapped her napkin in her lap.

He slowly lowered himself in the chair, and their arms touched. She shivered and glanced at J. J., but his eyes were lowered.

The doorbell rang, and Judd excused himself from the table to answer it. "Hi, Jack. Glad you could make it this morning. Food is on the serving table. Go help yourself." Jud looked helplessly at Karen for no one was showing up at the time they were supposed to arrive. Karen nodded, adding another place setting.

J. J. didn't eat, but he drank black coffee. Jud introduced everyone. Jack looked moon-eyed, and Claudia wore a silly grin on her face. Mariah sat daintily, holding her pinky up while eating, and J. J. jittered his leg, waiting on Jud's word so they could leave for the bank.

Jud gave Karen a brief kiss and saw her eyes twinkle. Grabbing his briefcase, he looked at J. J. and said, "You coming, boy?"

Scooting his chair back, he placed his napkin on the table, nodded, and excused himself. He put on his coat jacket, straightened his perfectly tied tie, and left with Jud.

Jud laughingly said, "That went well," as he put the car in gear.

Mariah said, "Claudia, why don't you step into the parlor?"

Following, Claudia blurted out, "I didn't know the ole fart would be here this morning."

Mariah answered, "Sometimes surprises are nice."

Puzzled, Claudia sat down.

"Claudia, Karen will join us in a minute."

Karen came into the parlor carrying a serving tray with cups of hot coffee. She said, "Mariah, Claudia will be fine this morning till early evening without a chaperone. Jack is filling in as the KD Bed-and-Breakfast lifeguard. He'll be downstairs with the twins and the new guests who are to arrive."

Mariah shook her head and placed a hand on Claudia's shoulder, "I'll be here early this evening. Why not plan to play a board game tonight like Monopoly, Clue, or Rummy?"

Claudia blinked her eyes and hit her leg, stating, "That sounds like a good idea."

Karen excused herself and went to the phone. She needed to call Jud. He was not available at the office, so Karen left a message with Miss Phyler. She said, "Let J. J. know he is to join the group this evening in playing board games."

Karen met Mariah as she wheeled from the room on her heels and tossed over her shoulder, "I'll see you tonight."

Mariah muttered something like, "This is not what I thought I had agreed to."

The cab honked twice. Mariah waved and then slid in, giving directions to the driver. The cabbie stopped in front of the local shop, and Mariah stepped into the building where she was to model hats. The scheduled event ran over, and she had to hurry to get to Karen's. She saw Claudia in her room as she passed by. She slowed down and lightly knocked on Claudia's door.

"Come in, Mariah. What did you do to your eyes? You're beautiful as a newborn calf."

Mariah paused and blushed. She was used to compliments and stares, but Claudia was so earthy, plain, and humble. Those qualities she hadn't known except in her brother, Ken. She told Claudia, "I'll hurry and change. Are jeans okay?" For the first time Mariah saw Claudia's face light up.

"Jeans it is," Claudia said, slapping her leg. "Let's meet in the parlor, say, in thirty-five minutes." She slapped Mariah on the back and closed the door.

Mariah spoke to herself while getting dressed. "Claudia is different from any person I've ever been around. Maybe this wasn't a good idea of me chaperoning her." What was the word she was looking for? "Um, Claudia is like an unpolished pearl in a clam. Well, you can't make a silk purse out of a sow's ear."

Mariah noticed Karen had placed ten chairs around the table in the parlor. And she had gathered several games for the guest to play if they chose. She brought in a plate of chicken salad finger sandwiches and included her specialty iced tea and a pot of fresh coffee. The side table held saucers, napkins, cups, glasses, and a bucket of ice. Karen had even arranged a tray holding cream, sugar, and lemon slices.

J. J. sat next to Jack. Both wore faded jeans and cotton shirts. The only difference between them was that Jack wore suspenders. Claudia appeared in bibs and lacy blouse. Mariah wore six-inch heels and designer brand jeans, which were rolled up at the bottom. She modeled a form-fitting top barely on her shoulders.

Karen asked, "Is there anything else I can do for you?"

Claudia tilted her head and belted, "No. Ain't you and Jud joining us?"

Karen smoothed her apron and warmly answered, "Maybe later" as she walked to the kitchen and continued to feed her husband and kids.

"Where's the guests? Our newlyweds?"

"Oh, Jud. Have you forgotten? They're due later." Karen blushed.

Jud blew Karen an airy kiss. "I love you."

Luke and Luci missed their nap, and Jud helped tuck Luke and Luci in bed after dinner while Karen read to them. She said, "Love you and lights out."

Jud nodded his head warmly in agreement, saying, "See you both in the morning." He ruffled Luke's hair and pulled Luci's nose.

Jud changed his business clothes to knee-length shorts and a pullover shirt. As Karen walked into the parlor, their eyes met. Jud motioned her to sit by him.

Karen refilled the tea pitcher and joined the group. She was distracted hearing Claudia and Jack talk about a puzzle piece and where it belonged. She watched as Jack guided Claudia's hand. She jumped at the sound when Mariah smacked J. J.'s hand from placing his piece into the puzzle. J. J. shot her a look and threw his piece down. Glancing up, he caught Jud's look and immediately squared his shoulders, muttering as Mariah placed her piece down, wearing the cat that caught the canary smile.

Two and a half hours passed, and only a few pieces were left before the five-hundred-piece puzzle was completed. Jack held Claudia's hand, and a romance seemed to be developing between them. J. J.'s demureness was strained. Karen noticed Mariah was not calm outwardly as she portrayed.

Mariah abruptly said, "Claudia, we ladies should call it an evening. Let's you and I take a brief walk?" She scooted from the chair and stated, "Men, if you'll excuse us."

Claudia eyed Jack, and Mariah interceded. "Jack, when will you be calling again?"

Jack faltered, but he soon recovered. Rubbing his hand on his jeans, he also stood up. "I would like to take Claudia out for an early dinner and catch a show tomorrow night. That is if Miss Claudia agrees?"

Mariah waited for Claudia to reply, but her mouth had opened. Claudia glanced at Mariah. Mariah straightened and held her hand out to Jack. "We'll be ready. Is five o'clock all right? Jack. Jack."

Reddening, Jack stuttered a humble, "Yes."

J. J. slapped Jack on the back and said, "That a boy. We'll be ready"

Mariah shot him a look.

Jud stood and said, "Karen, I'll lock up and check on the twins. You go on ahead to bed, and I'll catch up." He then walked Jack to the front door and bade him good night.

Karen felt her neck heat up and her face burn. It was so real as her first encounter with Jud. She stood up, straightened her skirt, and said, "I'll clean up in here. Ladies, J. J., I'll see you in the morning."

J. J. bowed from the waist and replied, "After you, ladies. I'll see you safely to your rooms."

Mariah clicked her heels a little too sharply as she assisted Claudia upstairs. The agitated glare passed from her to J. J. and melted as they held their gaze a bit too long.

Karen didn't know how Jud had pulled off the much-appreciated bubble bath, which awaited her. He was nowhere in sight when she slipped into the hot, inviting waters. She pulled her hair up and held it in place with two long pins. She slid her body down, resting her neck on the back of the tub. She waved her hands to move the waters over her. She loved the lavender oil and, oh, the bubbles. The smell drifted throughout the rooms. Finally relaxed and feeling like a prune, she stood and wrapped a bath towel around her. Her hair had come loose with a few tendrils around her face. She attempted to blow the strands from her forehead. She dressed in a frilly gown and matching robe. Karen pinched her cheeks as she slid into her feathered fluffy slippers.

When she stepped into the bedroom, there on the floor were yellow rose petals scattered all around. Her blue eyes followed the trail, and on the bed, Jud lay in his slacks with his hands behind his head, rose petals were surrounding him. Scented vanilla and lavender candles stood burning on the nightstands and the silk sheets were pulled back. Her jaw dropped. "Care to join me?" The corners of his mouth uplifted. .

Karen thought, *Oh, what a man!* She stared at his wedding ring and his wicked smile, noting how he still made her heart flutter. His smoky green eyes indicated desire as she stepped toward the bed. What a sight to behold. His abs were obvious and his arms flexed as he held them out for her. She reached her hand to his chest and she felt him quiver.

Jud scooted closer and nuzzled a kiss on the nape of her neck. "Karen, you are lovelier than the day we first met." He propped himself up, and the wantonness in his eyes said everything.

Karen moved closer, tilting her head and lingering for his kiss. "Jud, you are so sinful."

He replied with gentleness as their lips touched and slowly reached to unpin her hair. She felt the beat of his heart. There was strength and sweetness. They kissed again, and she felt alive. He whispered, "Stay with me," as he took the sheet and covered them.

She could not move. Karen was weak but was honored by his words. He snuggled closer, and she breathed a kiss on his ear and added, "Of course, my love." There in his arms, she awoke in the light of early morning. He had a tender smile as he gave her a kiss. As he edged from the bed she tugged at his tousled hair and pulled him unto her for another kiss. Time stood still.

It was now 6:30 a.m. Jud was finishing his black coffee. The bed-and-breakfast guests were seated at the table. J. J. made a combination sandwich of bacon and eggs. He swallowed his coffee and fanned his mouth after a drink of water. J. J. blotted his mouth and joined Jud in leaving for work.

Mariah said, "Claudia would you like spend time in Columbus? It's the capital. You can watch me model today then we could go shopping."

Claudia's face brightened and without hesitation replied, "Sure." Claudia scooted her chair back, and it screeched against the wooden floor. The ladies covered their ears, and Claudia said, "Sorry."

A cab was called, and soon Mariah and Claudia left for the city. Karen smiled. She was glad to have time alone with Luke and Luci. They made Jell-O desert with mixed fruit and made homemade whipped cream to add. And the twins brought out their coloring book. All was fine until Luke drew on on Luci's page.

She cried, "Look, Mom. He marked red on my silver star."

Before Karen could say anything, Luci scribbled on Luke's giraffe's neck, and it wasn't brown, black, or white. Words began. Luke grabbed her paper and tore it down the middle. Luci began crying. She grabbed his paper but stopped. Luke saw pain in his sister's eyes and began crying too. He said, in between hiccups, "I'm sorry, Luci, it was dumb to color red on your star and tear your coloring page."

Luci balled her hand into a fist. She reached for him and gave him a pop. Karen separated the twins and gave them a time-out. Jack came by and asked, "Anyone for a swim?"

Both twins looked from Jack to their mother waiting for an answer.

She looked down her nose. Karen asked, "Is all this bickering out of your system? Do you both feel better?"

The twins nodded their heads. Both answered in unison, "Yes."

Karen looked at Jack with a thankful smile and said, "Just an hour please."

While Jack agreed, he uttered, "Okay, you two, get your suits."

Karen said, "Help yourself to the fresh donuts, and I believe a cup or two of coffee is still left."

4

Sara glanced over her purse inventory. Different styles were sewn in the last month with help from her mother. Sara counted her stock—two hundred and twenty-three purses—which were now placed in boxes or hanging on display racks. She thought, *I wonder if Karen has enough purse inventory.* She made a call.

"Hello, Karen. It's Sara."

"Well, how are things?" Karen grabbed her planner and continued. "I was just ready to add up my two book shows." She sighed then asked, "Do you have any replacement purses available?"

"Yes, Karen. How many do you need and in which styles?"

After negotiating the styles and how many purses, Karen agreed to wire the money for the purses and the book sales. They talked a while longer and then Karen said, "Mother and Father left on another one of their voyages on the Atlantic. J. J. is here to help Jud at the bank upon orders from the redhead to clean up his act. Mariah is staying here while doing a modeling event at the hat store in Columbus. Oh, and Mariah agreed to chaperone Claudia. And Jack is acting like a kid at Christmas, courting." Karen hesitated then added, "Honestly, Sara, my head is spinning."

Sara tittered. "Can you figure the likes of Claudia and Mariah together?"

Karen muffled a giggle. "It's something all right, but they really get along amazingly."

Both ladies regained their control.

Sara cleared her throat and changed the subject. "Karen, did Jud mention anything to you about a bank conference there?"

Only a weak no was heard.

Sara said, "The New York meeting Jud was to attend was canceled, and he rescheduled. So Karen, Ken will be in Columbus soon, and Eurlene and Spencer is expected."

"What?" Karen gasped.

Sara said, "Karen, I can come with Ken and help you with shows or in the KD Bed-and-Breakfast. Mom can stay with Miechael and the boys. You remember Sam?"

"Why?"

"I think Mom has taken a liking to him. They seem to find time to talk, talk, talk. Sam will gladly help Mother with the boys."

Karen said, "Sara, you being here would be a godsend. There are guests coming in next week. And Claudia announced she's staying longer than planned. She really is a dear, but arrangements for her and Jack's courting have escalated."

Just then a chair screeched. "Sorry, Karen."

But Karen continued. "Mariah's modeling engagement was extended for another two weeks. And Sara, who knows how long it will take J. J. to get straightened out? Although he is very entertaining." Karen let out a heavy sigh. "You know this is the season the bed-and-breakfast business booms, and I have live book shows that are scheduled. Your help will be much appreciated."

Sara said, "It will be good to see you."

"And me, you. Thanks, friend."

Two weeks later, in mid-August, the weather was tortuous. Sara and Ken arrived at the KD Bed-and-Breakfast; it was dinnertime. Sara brought a shipment of purses and placed them on shelves in the office. It was like old times—Karen and her friend working in the kitchen.

Another honeymoon couple arrived a week earlier than originally planned. Karen handled everything in fashion while Jud handled the conversation. Karen bit her tongue when she observed the bride eyeing Jud. Although she seemed much in love with her husband and did hang on to his every word, Karen made a silent vow. "I need to spruce up and devote more time with Jud."

Karen in the kitchen recalled that arrangements were previously made for Claudia, Jack, Mariah, and J. J. to attend a dinner and a show.

Claudia's shopping adventure was to freshen up her wardrobe and style. Mariah and Claudia kidded with each other as they entered a large local women's clothing store. Claudia kept looking at the prices and saying, "Lads of mercy, this is pricey." She slapped her side.

Mariah suggested, "Claudia, try on this long black skirt and blouse." She also selected a loose sweater for a wrap. Claudia stared at herself in the mirror before walking out to show Mariah.

"Wow, Claudia, how attractive."

She nodded.

Mariah prompted, "Let's make your purchase. And Claudia, I'll treat you to a hair makeover."

"Oh, I couldn't, Mariah."

"Claudia, it's already arranged. I called Karen, and she made the hair appointment at the place where she used to work. Come on, it will be fun. Besides, when's the last time you've pampered yourself?"

Claudia hemmed and hawed, saying, "Well, my hair was colored eight months ago. A neighbor stopped by, and we put on different colors." Claudia's eyes narrowed. "I saw a movie star in a magazine with all these colors, and they were beautiful. Like a sun explosion."

Mariah noticed that Claudia was blushing. Mariah took Claudia's hand and led her through the store. She picked up a pair of low-slung heels to go along with her new selections. Claudia for once was speechless. Mariah entered the salon with Claudia, and everyone stopped working and just stared. Mariah squared her shoulders, tilted her head higher, and asked, "Which woman is Merrith? Don't just stand there staring." Mariah clicked her heel and waved. "I'm over here."

Merrith walked near the desk, chuckled, and addressed Claudia. "Sign in here, please."

Still tapping her foot, Mariah crossed her arms and locked eyes with Merrith. She did not expect any more words about Claudia's lack of beauty.

Claudia started fidgeting and shuffling her feet. Mariah placed a hand on her arm and nodded. "Its okay." She gave her a reassuring smile.

With newfound confidence, Claudia gracefully strutted with Merrith, saying, "Bring it on." She also received a manicure and a pedicure, her nails painted in a poppy red color.

Claudia, laughing, glanced at Mariah. "See my feet? Just look at my toes."

"I love the color," Mariah said warmly.

Claudia wiggled her toes and laughed. "My toes have cotton balls between them."

Mariah patted her hand. "Are you ready for your new hair adventure?"

"Well, my hair is thick and naturally curly." She lowered her eyes. "It's never been cut." Claudia's lip began to tremble.

Cheerfully, Mariah said, "Let's see the color wheel and get excited about these selections. We can ask Merrith her professional opinion on what would be suited for you. Okay?"

Shakily, Claudia nodded. She passed each color until she found "Somerset Red." Claudia leaped up. "I like this shade." She was beaming. Mariah walked over with Claudia and asked Merrith how it would look. Not waiting for an answer, Claudia said, "I want streaks of blond around my face."

Mariah consulted with Merrith about the choice of colors. After considerable thought, a decision was made. Merrith nodded and showed Claudia to the shampoo bowl. She placed a neck strip around her neck, added a towel, and covered her with a plastic cape.

After four and half hours, Claudia and Mariah headed for Karen's place. Claudia jabbed Mariah in the shoulder, saying, "Ain't my hair purty?"

Mariah smiled. "Claudia, we'll still have time to get ready before Jack arrives." They rushed up the steps, with Claudia taking two steps at a time. Thirty-three minutes later, the doorbell rang.

Mariah and Claudia watched from the top step as they waited on Jack's presence before coming down.

Jud greeted him. "Jack, old boy, you look like a brand new penny."

His smiled broadened. "Is Claudia ready? I bought her flowers. Think she'll like them?"

Jud nodded and turned to see why Jack's jaw dropped.

Claudia and Mariah descended the stairs.

They observed Claudia's hair and style. Her hair was surprisingly beautiful, lying in long ringlets past her shoulders. And she was wearing proper evening clothes. Jud chuckled lowly. Claudia, although a little wobbly, wore a slight heel.

Jud pushed himself forward and greeted Claudia. "Turn around and whirl so we can get a good look at you."

Jack held his hand out and offered the flowers, but his mouth was gaping. Claudia took the flowers and slapped Jack on the back. "Haven't you seen a girl all dolled up before?"

Mariah faced Jud, who was willing down a belly laugh.

"Claudia, our ride is waiting. Here, let me open the door for you, Claudia, Mariah." Jack guided her by the elbow.

"Jack, you're sitting too close. Scoot over. There's room for ten people in here."

Mariah whispered in Claudia's ear. "Jack is only being a respectful date to you, and he likes what he sees. And he wants to be near. Like a bee to honey."

"Oh." Claudia blushed and giggled, and then she looked at Jack. "There is pop in the refrigerator. I'll get you one." She placed a hand on the top of his knee.

"My, you had your nails done, too."

"Ah, Jack." She wiggled her right foot free from her shoe. "See? My toes. Yes, sir, they call it "poppy red." Ain't it purty?"

"Claudia, you are something else. Breathtaking, I say."

Mariah interjected with the name of the restaurant they would be going to and what play they would be seeing instead of a movie.

The chauffeur stopped and opened the door. He bowed as the ladies stepped out. Jack offered his arm willingly. Mariah took one side and nudged Claudia. She followed in suit and took his other arm. They stepped into the Southern Hotel. Claudia whistled. And in an outside voice said, "Look at all the glass hanging around the lights. Don't that beat all?"

Jack patted Claudia's arm and smiled.

Mariah's hazel eyes widened he saw the flash coming and pose.

Claudia stepped up and grabbed the camera. "Look, Bud, did we ask you for a picture taking?"

Jack pulled out a wad of money and handed it to the photographer. "That should be enough to cover your expenses." He walked faster. "Come Claudia, Mariah."

Jack moved to their table.

"Hi, Jack."

J. J. stood and waited for Claudia and Mariah to be seated.

"What are you doing here, J. J.?" Mariah spoke through clenched teeth, but she smiled when people looked their way. "Well?"

"So nice you could make it." Claudia dropped her jaw and winked.

Jack unfolded his napkin and watched Claudia put hers to her neck. He shook his head and nudged J. J. Jack loosened his tie and also placed his napkin at his neck. He thought, *Pick your battles. This napkin is no big deal.* His eyes were twinkling.

Mariah blew out a breath, snapped her napkin, and placed it on her lap. Her smile was plastered, and her jaws ached.

J. J. ran a finger around his collar. Mariah stared at him and asked, "J. J., are you attending the theater with us?"

He bit his lip. "Here, I remembered you like orchids. Might I add that you look fabulous, Mariah, just stunning as usual."

Jack, deep in conversation with Claudia, only paused long enough to pass the bread or ask for the salt. His full attention was on Claudia.

Mariah rolled up her sleeves and forked her food. Mariah felt a headache coming on, and the evening was just beginning.

J. J. was in a conversation with Jack and Claudia. He really appeared to be at ease with them. There wasn't any phoniness or wasted words. His black lined suit jacket was unbuttoned, and his arm was resting around a chair. He took time with the ladies who wanted to be photographed with him and gave them a handshake or a casual kiss on the cheek. A waitress slipped him what looked to be a phone number. He crossed over his hands and motioned back and forth and shook his head. His eyes were clear, and they enticed one into their blue depths.

These moments had shaken her. *Why did he needle me so much? We aren't even really friends. Why can't we have calm conversations instead of tit for tat?* She saw his gaze move over her. She blinked and placed the napkin on her plate. She cleared her throat. "Are we ready? The play begins in forty-five minutes. Our ride awaits us." She rose and touched Claudia's shoulder.

Jack reached for her chair.

"I can get up. Move, you old oaf." Claudia took his hand, but he led the way.

J. J. slid in before Jack and sat across from Mariah. Not a word was spoken from anyone. The car stopped in front the RKO, which seated over two thousand people.

Claudia looked up and then around. "I ain't been anywhere ever so fancy. Thanks, Mariah." She slapped Mariah on the back, causing her to lose balance and fall into J. J.'s path.

He automatically caught her by the waist. Mariah was relieved not to hit the ground. She glanced his way as he set her on her feet. His hands lingered on her arms. She shivered and bit her lip. Mariah forced herself to stay steady. "Thank you." She moved, and over her shoulder, she said, "Coming?" For a moment she saw vulnerability flickering in his blue eyes. She looked again, and they were concealed as he stepped her way.

During the play everyone knew what Claudia thought. She cheered, laughed, and even booed. The play ended, and everyone clapped and shouted with approval. Jack and J. J. stood and waited for Claudia and Mariah to join them. When they were riding in the limo, Claudia and Jack sounded like bees, but J. J. awkwardly stared out a window, only talking when asked a question.

Mariah willed herself to take an interest and remembered that she was chaperoning Claudia. She slipped glances toward J. J., but none were reflected back. The chatter was there. On the outside, she was formal and polished, but inside she quivered. She hadn't felt so alone in such a long, long time. She pinched her arm, keeping her in the here and now. Mariah refused to be seen as vulnerable. She slipped the driver money and took hold of Claudia's arm, saying, "Men, we bid you farewell." She instructed Claudia by nodding.

Claudia slapped Jack on the arm and said, "Thanks, Jack, for the date."

Mariah said, "Call us, Jack." The ladies entered the house. But not J. J.

The smell of Karen's breakfast wafted under the guests' noses. Everyone was seated except J. J. Mariah listened, joked, and even shared food with the guests; she also helped Claudia. She was very surprised when Ken and Sara appeared. Her hands flew to her heart. "Is Miechael with you?"

"No, Mariah. Grandmother Louise is caring for him and the boys." Laughing, Ken added, "And Sam."

"How's he doing? What are you doing here?"

"Good to see you too." Ken swung Mariah around. "I'm here on bank business, and Sara is here to help Karen out with her shows. We're only here for two days. How's modeling working out?"

Mariah's smile widened. She kissed Ken's cheek and hugged Sara. "The little hat shop extended my contract for another two weeks. And Karen graciously made room for me."

Ken's ebony eyes glistened. "I'm glad things are working out." He lowered his voice. "Isn't Claudia something?" A smile formed and lifted the corners of his lips.

"Ken?" She stomped her foot.

"What?"

"How's my boy?"

"He's adjusting nicely to country living and he seems to be enjoying himself. Ken reached into his jacket pocket and said, "Mariah here's some recent pictures of Miechael roping and riding a horse."

Mariah grabbed the pictures. "Thanks."

Ken raised his arms in defeat. Turning, he noticed Jud motioning. He gave Sara a light kiss and nodded to Mariah as he walked toward Jud.

Mariah heard their conversation. "Ken, let's get to the office and join the others. No J. J. is there." She saw that Jud cuffed Ken on the arm before they exited.

She returned her attention back to Sara and Claudia. She raised her brows and asked, "Ladies, board games tonight?"

Karen nodded. She knew she was into a long night.

Mariah sipped her tea then stood up. She said, "It's time for me to dress for my modeling engagement." She rolled her eyes and laughed.

5

Karen and Sara looked over the book shows, which arrived through the mail. Both ladies took turns entering the data in the computer and jotting down the new hostesses' names. Karen tapped her pencil as she called each person, asking for his or her address and finding out what style of purse the hostess desired. Then she and Sara prepared hostess packages and placed them in the outgoing mail.

The phone rang, and Karen booked two suites for the following month.

Sara rose and took Karen by the arm. "Let's take a break. Then we'll get lunch for the tribe and the guests. Come on, let's go for a walk."

As Karen and Sara walk on the path, the air filled with the sweet smell of magnolia, and Honeysuckle. Karen found her spirit feeling lighter, and she said, "Sara, thanks for coming. What a friend."

"You're welcome, Karen. But I must say that I have news to share with you." Sara placed her hands to her mouth. She lowered her voice and whispered in Karen's ear, "I'm pregnant."

"What?" A smile spread across Karen's face. "When are you expecting?"

"The later part of spring. Karen, look, I'm carrying this one differently. Maybe it's a girl!"

The ladies hugged. Karen turned pink and said, "Sara, I too am pregnant. I'm so happy, but Jud doesn't know yet. I just found out yesterday. I'm trying to hide the baby bump until he and I are romantically alone."

They hugged some more and danced. Their eyes were brightly lit with happiness.

The dinner rush was finally over, and enough potatoes were left to make a potpie. Karen gathered the other ingredients and prepared for the next meal. Sara fixed a garden salad and placed it in the refrigerator. She saw that Karen had made plenty of her special mint chocolate iced tea.

Sara left for a purse show so Karen could stay home and play board games with her guests as well as Mariah, Claudia, and Jack. Karen went to the kitchen and brought back tea and coffee along with sweetened rolls. After a few games, Karen retired the twins to their rooms, where she read to them. She kissed and tucked Luke into his bed then walked Luci to her room.

Karen thought, *Mother's due back from vacationing and she asked for the kids.* She let out a long sigh. "Finally, I'll get to be alone with my husband. We need to talk." She drew a bubble bath and hummed. Karen added lavender salts and slid into the tub. When she awoke, there was only a soft light filtering under the bathroom door. The bubbles were gone, and the water was cold. She shivered. Karen quickly dried off and reached for her old nightclothes, but she changed her mind and entered her closet and pulled out a newly bought nightwear ensemble, a red flowing gown with a matching robe.

She walked gracefully into the bedroom. Jud's eyes were closed, but when she sat on his side of the bed and stroked his face, his green eyes opened and flashed wickedness. He pushed the sheet back and scooted over. She reached his shoulders and gave him a light kiss. Leaning in to meet his full lips, she asked, "Can we get away soon? Have a few days to ourselves?"

Jud half sat and traced her mouth with a finger. "Why, sweetheart?"

Karen placed her arms around him and nestled her fingers in his hair. He reached for the tie holding her robe closed. The phone rang. She motioned to him to answer the phone. He jumped from the bed, grabbed his robe, and slammed into his slippers.

"Hello, this is Jud. Who's calling, please?"

Hi, Jud. This is Sam. Sorry about the lateness."

"What's wrong?"

"Jud, I need to speak with Ken. And nothing is wrong. Everything is fine."

Jud heard giggling on the other end. "Wait a minute, and I'll get Ken."

Karen had changed and joined her husband. "Who is it? Anything wrong?"

"Go back to bed, Karen." Jud spoke a little harshly. "Nothing is wrong. Sam wants to speak with Ken."

A faint knock came at the door. Ken opened the door slightly and rubbed his eyes. "Jud, what's wrong?" Not waiting for an answer, he put on his robe, picked up his slippers, and eased out the door.

"Sam wants to talk with you on the phone. He said nothing is wrong. I'm sorry to, umm, bother your sleep."

Ken ruffled his hair. "You seem upset, my friend."

"Not really, just working too hard. I think Karen and I are soon taking a much needed holiday."

"Hello, Sam? You what? When? You old dog."

Karen put on a pot of coffee and placed a heated snack on the table. She knew by Jud's tone that he was troubled.

Sara joined them, saying, "I smelled the coffee."

Jud half smiled. "Karen, thank you."

She nodded. "Cream, sugar?"

Sara touched Ken's sleeve. "Who called at this hour? And what did they want?"

"Calm down. Let's pray."

Sara bounced her head up. "Well, what?"

"It was Sam on the line. The children are fine, but he and your mother have a surprise for you."

"Tell me."

Ken looked at Jud and Karen, and he opened his hands to Sara and stared. "Sam proposed to your mother, and she accepted. A circuit judge came to our town, and they are now hitched."

Jud shook his head. Karen sat down and placed a hand on Sara's arm. Sara plopped down with her mouth wide open. *Mom and Sam—married.*

Morning came. The guests were deep in conversation while fixing their breakfast plates. Most guests had booked a suite for the following year to celebrate their anniversaries or a planned getaway. Some needed a ride to the airport, and Karen made arrangements by calling them a cab.

J. J. edged nearer to Jud and had a long talk concerning his feelings for Mariah. He also quoted what Ken had said: "Help Mariah, but hands off my sister. She's a real lady."

Jud strummed his chin and then advised, "J. J., my man, you need to talk with Ken and be honest. Think out your thoughts before speaking." Jud placed a hand on his shoulder. "J. J., how do you think Mariah feels about you?"

"I really don't know. She shows interest in me, but there's no follow through. She keeps away or makes disgusted looks at me. She's a hard one to figure out."

"What about her son? How well do you know him?"

"Jud, it's hard to express myself when Ken objects to me, and don't forget how my sister runs my life."

"J. J., here's my advice. Take it to heart. Give you and Mariah some space or time apart from each other. Get to really know her son, Miechael. Volunteer to work for Ken at the bank again.

You would be away from Mariah and would be seriously able to search out all your feelings and desires. Ken and Miechael will draw closer to you for they will know you better. Now through prayers, you'll have your answer if Mariah turns out to be your one and only. Eurlene and Ken will come around."

J. J. clasped Jud in a sound hug. "Thanks, sir."

Ken entered the room, eating a bite of toast and cupping his coffee. He looked at both men. "Why so serious?"

Jud said, "Let's go talk bank business." He glanced at J. J.

Claudia entered the room, saying her farewells. "It's time to head home for the ranch. My vacation time from the hospital has ended." She withdrew her handkerchief and blew. "In a few hours, Jack and I will say good-bye."

The day at the park was wonderful. Mariah, Claudia, and Jack went on a walking trail. They collected rocks from the creek's edge. And under a partially hidden tree, Jack held Claudia's arms and gave her a little smooch.

Mariah cleared her throat. "Claudia, thanks for letting me have a part in your and Jack's courtship."

"Shucks. I'm glad you're here, hat model."

Mariah chuckled. "Jack, you are such a warm and kind being. It's nice to have met someone who lives for the Lord."

Jack nodded then asked, "Mariah, have you ever thought of giving yourself personally to Him?"

Mariah patted Jack's shoulder. "Maybe, but not now."

Jack looked at Claudia. "I can't come to the airport to see you off for I am scheduled to speak at a seminar. Will you be all right without my being there? I'll fly and come to your place before the year is over. It's only three months."

Claudia lifted him up and plopped a kiss on his lips. She took her long hanky from her bib pocket and blew her nose. "Old goat, I'll be waiting."

Jack took a few steps, getting his balance. "Come on now, let me hug you." He wrapped his arms around her until his fingers met. He squeezed her, and a tear dropped. She pushed away and bent over, catching her breath. Jack kneeled. "Claudia, I love you."

Mariah gasped then held her breath, watching Jack. She glanced in Claudia's direction and waited.

Claudia ogled Jack then grabbed his arm. "Get up." With hands on her hips, she added, "Jack, it's too soon for me to know how I feel." Old thoughts rush in her mind how long a go a guy she had hopes in marrying dumped her. Claudia looked up and slapped him on the back. "Call me if you want. Now let's not get all sentimental going our separate ways." She blew her nose again.

Jack look intently in disbelief. "Claudia, I'll call, and I will come to your farm. You aren't getting rid of me."

Claudia hit her leg with her straw hat and said, "I'll be there. Have a safe trip. See ya." She turned and looped her arm in Mariah's. "It's time to be heading out, sugar."

Mariah shook her head and said, "Claudia, I'm catching the same flight as you, but I'm going on to my brother's place to see my boy." She silently thought, *I have ten days of holiday left before starting another photo shoot in New York and then I'll deal with the sad state of my New York suite.*

"Mother." Miechael bowed. "It's so good to see you. Is there a troubled matter?"

"No. Only I've missed you terribly, and I have a few days I can spend with you. I'm in between my modeling assignments." Mariah touched his cheek. "You are quite handsome in your clothes. I like the boots."

"Uncle Ken isn't here right now. He had business dealings with Jud, but Sam is here. Mother, Sam and Louise got married. It was so interesting. A real country judge came here to the farm, and we—Timmy, Matthew, and I—watched the ceremony. We had front-row seats. Louise giggled a lot, and Sam had a wide smile, and it's still on his face. Old people are so funny, don't you think?"

"Miechael, they are called mature grown-ups. Please don't use the expression 'old,' all right?"

"Sorry."

Mariah gave him a big hug then distanced herself. "I'm going in to talk with Louise. Are you helping out with your cousins?"

"Mother, we help each other, and Sam is great with us. Besides, Uncle Ken and Aunt Sara will be here soon. It's good to see you, Mother." He reached for her hand and gave it a kiss.

Mariah bit her bottom lip. She felt him pulling away. She started for the house.

"Mother?"

Mariah turned. Miechael ran to her and wrapped his arms around her waist. "I love you, Mommy."

She hung on to him, took off his hat, and messed up his dark hair, which was well in need of a haircut. "I love you too, and I have missed you."

"Mother, may I stay here and attend school instead of attending school abroad? I have a letter from Grand Ma Mere, and she is coming to Ken's next week about my schooling."

Mariah's lips went thin. "We'll see about schooling."

Turning, she found Louise standing in front of the baked goods, which were lined on the counter. Louise was covered with flour.

"Hello, Louise. I understand best wishes are in order to you and Sam. Are you happy, Louise?"

She appeared to be floating on the clouds. Louise wiped her hands on her apron and put her hands to her cheeks, as if that would ward off the blush from her neck and face. Louise took a deep breath. "I am happy." She turned and handed Mariah a cup of hot tea. "One lump or two, and here's the cream and lemon. Dinner is at six. Don't be late. Maybe you would like a rest before we eat. And Mariah, thanks for asking about Sam and me." Louise turned again and began peeling potatoes.

Mariah awoke to noise, which drifted to her room. She heard the boys speaking, and they were not in agreement. She also heard men's voices, and they sounded happy. Mariah quickly showered and saw that she had twenty minutes to make it down to the dinner table. She strummed through her clothes and decided on a light blue sheath and low heels. She adjusted her fake eyelashes and added a touch of peach blush. She reddened her lips and powdered her nose. She looked into the mirror, and the reflection was smiling back. She felt really rested and in unusually high spirits as she waltzed into the kitchen.

There stood J. J. hanging out with Ken and Sam. Her stomach took a plunge. Ken had just cuffed Sam on the sleeve, and J. J. was bending over, it seemed, from laughter.

She willed her fists to her sides and smiled as Miechael offered her a seat. J. J. turned, and his smile disappeared. Sam helped Louise set the table, and then everyone was seated. Ken asked for each person to hold hands as he said the blessing.

Miechael looked gloomy. Mariah asked, "Son, what's the matter?"

He blurted out, "Timmy said Sam is not my grandpa."

"He's not. He's mine and Matthew's."

"Yea. Mine and Timmy's."

"Boys." Louise called to Timmy. "Now I want you to understand we all are family."

Sam spoke up. "Miechael, step over here please."

Miechael slung his head back and stood before Sam. "Son, we spoke about love, family, and friendships, have we not?"

"Yes, sir, but—"

"No buts." Sam placed his arm around Miechael's shoulders. "When your great-grandparents, the Duke and Lady Ma Mere called, making a point of speaking only with you, not the other boys, how do you think Timmy and Matthew felt? Although they are somewhat correct, family should be family even to the extended members."

Miechael held his head down, and tears slipped from his eyes. "I'm sorry, Sam. I don't want to be a stuffy and self-absorbed person."

"I know, my boy, and you can call me Grandpa if you like. It has a nice ring to it." Sam stood and hugged Miechael. Then he included Timmy and Matthew. "Well, boys, can we share me?"

Timmy scooted his chair and so did Matthew, and then a crash happened. Matthew picked up his chair and joined Timmy in hugging Miechael. "Me too."

A smile broadened on Miechael's face as he picked Matthew up. "We're family." He looked at his mother. "Isn't that right, Mother?"

Mariah was holding her breath trying to compose herself, but her jaw had dropped at this outburst. She had mixed feelings exploding through her. She was surprised, happy, and sad all at the same time. She mustered a smile. She tried to eat, but the hunger had passed. She stirred her food and attempted to fork a bite. It tasted like cotton, and even water did not wash the food down. She excused herself and motioned for Miechael to join her.

Mariah sat beside her son on the back porch swing. "Miechael, I'm so very proud that you, even being aristocratic, are not spoiled. You have great leadership abilities." She ruffled his hair. "You're a lot like your loving father and your uncle Ken. Seeing how you were today, I will talk with my brother about you attending public school this year, but"—she pointed a finger—"it's for this year only, then for the next three years, you will study abroad. I want you to come home every holiday, or I'll come to you. Do you understand and agree?"

"Oh, Mother." Miechael flung his arms around her, tipping his hat off. "Mother, I would wish to graduate school from here, but I'll accept a year, thank you. You need to be here and really get to know Aunt Sara and Uncle Ken. They are great people."

She turned and was surprised to see J. J. standing in the doorway. "Miechael, go play or help out with your cousins," she said.

6

"Mariah, may we talk?" His voice cracked. His magnetic blue eyes lingered.

"J. J., we have nothing to talk about." She crossed her arms. "I didn't know you would be here or I wouldn't come. I'll leave by morning. But you, stay as long as they will have you." Mariah squared her shoulders, smoothed her dress, and turned to walk away.

She looked at Ken as he slipped his arm around her. "Sis, I'm so glad you're here. I do want to know you better as Sara does. Please stay for a while. And when the Grand Ma Mere comes, I'm going to need help. What do you say?" He hung on tightly, and his dark eyes silently pleaded with her.

"Ken, let loose of me. You're wrinkling my clothes."

He laughed but loosened his grip.

"I will stay a few days and help you battle the Duke and Lady, but I doubt you'll need any of my help." She took his arm and moved a few steps. "I do want to speak with you about Miechael's schooling."

"Great, sis. I have a few chores waiting, and I have business with J. J. Can we get together tomorrow morning?"

Mariah nodded. "My name is Mariah." She stiffened and walked back inside.

"Mariah, come with me," Sara said as she held out her hand. Mariah slid her hand in Sara's and smiled. They walked into Sara's office. "Look, Mariah, I made these for you." She held up three purses—a red, a black-striped, and a bright-colored paisley one.

Mariah's hazel eyes widened. Nothing had ever been given to her unconditionally. She sniffed and said, "Sara how beautifully made these purses are." The tears fell. Unexpectedly, Mariah wrapped her arms around Sara.

Ken wandered toward the barnyard and saw Sara's mother. He said, "Mom, what are you doing out here in the barn?"

Louise blushed. "Well, Ken, this is where I'm going to stay with Sam."

Ken shoved his hat back and placed his hand on Sam's back. "Sam, you stay in the house with Louise. We'll work out everything, okay? We're family."

Sam dusted off his chaps and smiled. "Ken, Louise sit down." Both sat on a bale of straw and looked at each other. The boys had wandered off, heading toward the house for a late snack.

"Ken, Louise, it's time you both know I have a ranch that was left to me in the next county over. It's vacant except for an artist who stays in the small bungalow on the property. The ranch belonged to my father, who left it to me. I was abroad when he passed away. When I arrived at the farm, the attorney handed me an order for the specialty cattle my father raised. I contacted the gentleman requesting the order, and after one week, I traveled by train with the cattle to their new settlement. The amount paid was unheard of. The attorney advised me that before I decided to sell the farm, I should take time and pray for God's will. That's how I happened here at your place, Ken, three years ago."

Louise batted her eyes, and Ken's eyebrows were scrunched. "Ken, this may come as a shock, but I have money, lots of it. What you paid me, I've invested back into my farm. I hired a young ranch hand, who managed the farm. And he added on more ranch hands."

Louise, surprised, only muttered, "My goodness. Sam, I didn't think I would have to leave my grandchildren." She placed her arms around him and gathered him closely. "Sam, I never suspected anything. Let's pray. I'm sure He holds the answers." They kneeled, held hands, and offered up a prayer for thankfulness, help, and guidance.

J. J. sat at the kitchen table playing checkers with the boys. He played the winner from Matthew and Timmy. He sat another checker game out and had Miechael playing a game with him.

He had helped himself to some snacks, and he also gave the boys milk and chocolate chip cookies. They all were joking and had crumbs everywhere.

Louise went to place on her apron, as Sam motioned her not to. She looked and saw Mariah and Sara enter, and she nodded to Sam. They slipped from the kitchen into her room.

Miechael stood to sit with his mother, but she waved him off and sat down, watching. Sara joined, and Matthew said, "Play, Aunt Mariah."

Sara played against J. J. and Timmy against Mariah. Sara lost and so did Timmy. Sara said, "Mariah, you play J. J. and win, please. Save face for me."

Sara walked from the room. "Come, boys, bedtime."

"Come on, Miechael, Mom will read to us."

The scampering of feet was all J. J. and Mariah heard.

"Okay, Miss Show-Off. I'm taking you down."

"Says who? The Peanut Gallery?"

"Good one. Crown me." He quickly covered his head. "The checker. Okay, you have a win. Let's play best two out of three. Ouch, Mariah, you won again. Would you like to help me make a cheese-and-pepperoni pizza?"

"I can almost taste it. Do they have any Coke?"

J. J. hesitated but only for a moment. He turned toward Mariah and asked, "So, how did you manage to raise such a wonderful young man?"

Mariah heart softened. Her mind travelled to another time earlier in her life. And almost in a whisper, she said, "Joshua, about my first husband, Miechael's father, was a terrific man and meant everything to me. We met while I, a student, attended college in Europe. He, the professor, and I, one of his students. Four years later, after my graduation, the professor contacted me, and after a few dates, we married. It was such an impulsive decision. And the professor and I enjoyed a blissful three days together." Her lips quivered. She continued. "He was in an accident on his way home to me and died before I got to the hospital." Mariah sighed. J. J. sat very still.

Clearing her throat,-"The hospital called my Grand Ma Mere. I was all alone and young. They came and nursed me back among the living. The Ma Meres had legal papers designed for me to carry my maiden name, and then they contacted my mother, Sylvia, but everything was hush, hush—nothing was mentioned about my professor being my husband." Mariah let out a long breath.

"Mother was only informed that I would be traveling with her parents for a while. During the cruise I discovered from the cruise doctor that my sickness wasn't from the sea but that I was, shockingly, pregnant. I swore the doctor to secrecy and later sent for my records. Eight months later at my flat, in Europe, the Grand Ma Mere made a surprise visit. She had knocked on the door, it opened, and she came in. I was holding Miechael. One look at him and she knew who the father was."

J. J. reached for Mariah's hand and looked into the the softness of her eyes. He said, "Mariah, I'm truly sorry for your loss and all the loneliness you must have experienced."

Ken entered the room. "The oven, it's smoking."

Together, they both answered. "It's pizza." Then there was laughter.

Ken sat down and unfolded a napkin. "Well?"

Mariah struggled, but she managed to cut the pizza in slices. J. J. placed the pizza on plates and carried it to the table. J. J. and Mariah both licked their fingers and continued playing their third game of checkers. "I win. You lose. I told you so."

"Well, champ," Ken motioned. "Stay seated. Now, see the pro."

Mariah placed her fingers on Ken's shoulders, and he patted them.

"J. J., king me. Again, J. J., I can't hear you." Ken was bent with amusement. It was a balmy September day. The leaves had mostly fallen, and the children were playing on their mounts. Sam had fixed a grilled breakfast when the phone rang. Ken answered, "Hello. Sara and Ken Newses' residence."

"Ken, it's me, Spencer."

"You sound far away. Are you back in Rome?"

"No. We are in Spain. I need you to conference Jud to our line."

"Hang on." There was a click and a ring.

"Hello?"

"Hello, Jud. I have Spencer on the other line. He wants to speak with both of us." The lines crackled. "Hello, Spencer. Here's Jud? I'm here too. So Spencer, what's going on?"

"Eurlene and I are getting married. And we want you, Ken, and you, Jud to bring your wives and come to Spain. And Jud, I want you to be my best man. Now how do I get in touch with J. J. and Mariah? I've tried both their numbers, but nobody answers. I just get their machines."

Ken quickly spoke. "They are both here at the farm. I'll get them. Hold on."

Mariah placed the receiver to her ear. "Hello?"

"This is Eurlene. I would appreciate your influence here in Spain. I must shop for a wedding gown, and quite frankly, I like your style. Since you have frequently traveled in this country, please come and help me."

Eurlene took a quick breath. "Mariah, place J. J. on the line!"

"I'm here."

"J. J., you travel with Mariah and no silliness. I want you to walk me down the aisle, brother. You and Mariah need to be here in two weeks. Now put Ken and Jud on the line!"

Ken pushed the speaker button back on and said, "Jud and I are here."

Eurlene said, "Ken, Jud, you'll need to arrive here three weeks from today! The hotel will have all your reservations. Ciao."

Chuckling was heard in the background as Spencer came on the line. "Jud, Ken, isn't she something? Oh, I love her so. See you in three weeks, men. Bye."

"Spencer, Spencer?" The line crackled and went silent.

"Jud, you still there?"

"I am, but I can't go! Who would handle the bank business?"

"You know Miss Phyler is quite capable of handling the bank. It would be like a honeymoon for us, my friend. I'm sure Karen would love Spain."

"Right. I know Karen. Are you kidding at Eurlene's wedding? That's asking for trouble."

"Jud, it's Spencer and Hot Thing." He couldn't control the laughter.

"What are you going to do about your farm and the bank, Ken?"

"I'll talk with Sam. Wait till you hear the news about him. He's highly educated and wealthy! Louise and Sam seem really suited for one other. She seems so happy, and he dotes on her. I'll catch up with you later. I need to work out some things about the bank, and you need to prepare Karen. You better pray a lot." Ken cleared his throat. "I'll talk with you in a day or so or send you an e-mail. Bye, Jud."

"Bye."

Ken entered the kitchen to see a pot holder whiz by. "Hey, what's going on in here? J. J., do you wish to explain?"

"Why do you always think the worst of me?"

"Well, do you think it would be my sister?" He teased, "I don't think so." Ken laughed. Ken's creases by his mouth were turning up. "J. J., get ready. We are leaving for the bank." He turned and took Mariah's hand and walked her to Sara's office. "I think she needs your help." Ken nodded at Sara. He brushed her lips lightly and whispered, "Help, she's wild."

Sara said, "Honey, have a nice day. Mariah and I are going on a purse show."

She looked at Mariah, her forehead furrowed. "You remembered us planning the show, don't you?"

"Not really, Sara. You sure we talked?"

"Come on, we'll wear suits, and on the way I'll go over the plan with you. We'll have fun. Mom's having a picnic with the boys, and they are going fishing in the creek. Sam will be joining them. Get a move on it, Mariah. Meet you in the truck."

Ken knew Sara won that round, so he quietly walked to his car. J. J. stood up, properly dressed and waiting with briefcase in hand.

Mariah was surprised at how accepted she was with the town ladies. During the order process, they asked Mariah for tips on attractiveness. Mariah showed the crowd the purse Sara had made and gave them additional reasons for the ladies to purchase for themselves. Sara noticed her sales were up, and so were the bookings.

On the ride home, they stopped at the local drugstore's soda fountain. Sara paid and thanked Mariah for her creative help. "The ladies loved you and your tips. My, what lady wouldn't want to look like you or wear things like you do. I'm impressed."

"It will be good for the products I model, and honestly, Sara, I've never cared before."

"It's family. We're growing on you."

"I guess."

They finished their milkshakes and entered the car.

The radio station was switched, and singing was at the top of their lungs. They met Louise in the kitchen, sipping a cup of tea. "The tea is hot. Would you like to join me, Sara, Mariah?"

"Sure."

Mariah asked, "How were the boys?"

Sara took a sip and added another lump of sugar. "Did they catch any fish?"

Louise began giggling. "I'm glad the night air had warmth in it for the fishing was ditz. Instead, Sam tossed the boys in the creek, and he plunged in afterwards. They had so much fun. All four were mud balls from head to toe."

Miechael said, "The Grand Ma Mere pays for her mud baths." It was so funny.

Mariah began laughing and tried to speak, but she could only slap her knee. Sara and Louise joined her. They laughed until they cried.

Sara said, "My sides hurt." She burst out laughing again.

Mariah took a deep breath, willing down the chuckles, but Ken and Sam entered the room and the laughter started all over again.

Ken motioned to Sam, and he shook his head. But he wanted a good laugh, so Sam sat down and took Louise's hand. Ken followed suit. "Well, ladies, I see you are having a good time."

The ladies nodded in unison. Mariah tried to explain, but it wasn't as funny to the guys as it still was to the ladies. They finished their tea and agreed it was time to turn in.

7

Swooping Sara up, Ken gave her a kiss before letting her down on the bed.

"What was that for? Mind you, I'm not complaining, Ken!"

"Good," he spoke from the bathroom. Ken padded to the bed and kneeled for his nightly prayers. He felt warmth as Sara placed her hand on top of his. "Dear Lord, thank You for us, the children, and the family we're in. Thank You, for Your Son, and for our salvation. Your goodness is gracious and kind. Be with us through the night, your humble servant, Ken."

He rose, and she stood with him. He bent and lightly embraced her, and her lips warmed him. He pulled back the sheet and patted the bed. She slid in, patting the area beside her. He nodded and shut the door closed it tightly with his foot.

The moonlight was softly filtering in through the window. Ken placed his head on his hand and spoke softly to Sara. "I received a phone call yesterday from Spencer. It seems that he's caught Eurlene, or it may have been vice versa. Anyway, he has asked her to marry him, and while they are still in Spain, she has agreed."

"Oh, how romantic."

"Sara." He brushed her lips lightly and said, "They want us to come and take part in their wedding celebration. We can go. I talked to Sam, and with his knowledge and background, he will take care of the bank business and help Louise with all three boys. We could have a wonderful time ourselves." He touched her cheeks and let his fingers trail.

Sara shivered.

Ken whispered, "Sara."

She sat up. "When would we leave? How long will we be there? Oh, and we need passports and—"

"Sara." He kissed her and laid her down.

He carefully moved from the room as she slept. He left a note.

> Sara, schedule your purse shows for the last of next month.
> I'll take care of our passports. See you tonight, love.
>
> Ken

Sara worked in her office all morning, moving and shuffling her scheduled purse shows. Her mother walked in, and Sara glanced up. "Mom, I love you, and I know you are really happy. Sam is such a good man, but he's blessed to have you too."

Louise dabbed her eyes, and both women hugged.

"Sara, you'll need to leave me a list of any allergies the boys may have and their doctor's and dentist's names along with their numbers. Do they have limits in any sports? Sara, I want you to have fun and fall in love with Ken all over again." She patted Sara's tummy. "Oh, it would be nice to dote on a little girl."

Sara nodded and blushed.

Back at the Day household, Jud asked, "Karen when are your parents due back from their travel?"

"Jud, they will be here this evening. I'm making Dad's favorite: meatloaf." She frowned then added, "I want you here at a decent hour. We miss you."

Jud took in a breath. "Karen, I love you. I like meatloaf."

"I'm fixing a mix peach cobbler, and we are having homemade ice cream."

"You're awesome, Karen." He closed in and held her tightly. "Honey, I want to talk with you tonight. It's important to me."

"Okay. Dinner is at six. Then we can play a board game. What do you say?"

"I'll be here, and let the games begin." He smiled wickedly and slapped her on her rump as he went out the door.

He found himself deep in conversation and work with Miss Phyler. She had a custom of handwriting all business matters down. All forms, letters, and conversations. Her work took longer, but she was exact and precise on all matters. She was thrilled to find out she was in charge of the bank. She said, "Jud, you believe in me as did your father, Mr. Tom Day."

She promised to practice emailing. Every day until the date of their departure, she struggled but continued to wear a smile. On the day before leaving, Jud said his good-byes. "I'll bring you a back a hat, Miss Phyler." He smiled.

She pointed a long, skinny index finger up at him. "Take time and show Karen how special she is. Amour." Miss Phyler walked away from the office, tapping her notebook.

Jud hurried home, carrying a massive bunch of flowers.

Karen blushed. "Thanks." She placed them in a vase, adding water and an aspirin. She set the floral arrangement on the dinner table for everyone to see. Jud had washed up, and he came to the table. "Good evening, Donald, Kate. It's nice to have you back with us. Looking forward to hearing about your trip."

He glanced Karen's way and asked, "Do you need any help."

Luci said, "No, thank you, Daddy. I'm assisting Mother."

"What are you doing, Luke?"

"Waiting on Mother to sit down. I am pushing in her chair. I saw Miechael helping his mother."

"Oh, I see. You both are so grown-up." His dimple appeared on his right cheek.

Everyone was seated, a prayer was said, and the food flowed; it tasted great. Jud asked for seconds of the cobbler. After dinner, Jud cleared the table, and Kate got coffee and iced tea and brought them to the game table. They played Rummy 500 and no three-of-a-kind were allowed.

Luci squealed when she reached five hundred first. Karen then mentioned it was time for bed. She asked Luke to pick out the story that she would read.

Jud took the opportunity to speak with Karen's mother and father about the trip and why they needed to attend Attorney Spencer and Eurlene's wedding in Spain. "Will you watch the twins for a couple of weeks? Beginning soon?"

"Jud what does Karen think?" Her mother's eyes widened.

Jud cleared his throat. "Karen doesn't know."

"Know what, Jud?"

He wheeled around, spilling some coffee.

Karen's father motioned for her to sit beside him. "Jud was just about to tell us of Spencer and Eurlene's upcoming wedding."

"What? When is this happening?"

All eyes were on Jud. He felt the pressure. He looked upward and silently spoke to God. *Give me wisdom as I speak. Thank you, but help in a hurry would be nice.*

In slow motion, Jud pulled out a chair and sat down. He looked at Donald, Kate, and Karen. "I received a call from Ken and was connected in a conference call with Spencer. Spencer is now in Spain." Jud took a sip of coffee and looked around. His green eyes narrowed as he spoke. "Spencer announced the wedding plans and asked for us—you and me, Karen—to come and be part of their wedding celebration. He wants me to be his best man, and we are to leave in two and a half weeks." He sighed.

Donald spoke up. "This is a very important act, I can see, from the business aspect." Holding a hand up, he continued. "Sweet Karen, this would be a good time for you to put away the green-eyed monster once and for all."

Karen squirmed, and Jud muffled a laugh.

Kate took the hint and stood up. "Karen, we'll need to do some shopping." Kate turned her head. "Jud, how long will you and Karen be gone?"

"What? Don't I have a say in this matter?" Karen pushed her chair back, and they fell silent.

Jud proceeded to her and reached for her shoulders. Karen took a step backward and turned. Her face was heated. She willed her fisted hands to her sides. "I'm not a child. I don't mean to be, but I'm a little jealous of you, even seeing Eurlene! After all there is quite a history between the two of you. How do I know that, that red head will go through with a wedding to Spencer?"

Jud moved closer. "Now, Karen. Come on. You know you're the only woman for me, and no, you're not a child." He leaned closer and lowly whispered, "But you can use me as a play toy." He stroked her arms. "I want us to attend, and I want time to be alone with you. Please come with me. First, it's for Spencer, my business attorney. And second, it's for us. With a beautiful country and a lovely woman, my wife by my side, we could be in so much trouble."

Karen could not fight his whimsical and loving ways. She caved. "Mother, if Dad can watch the twins, we can take the Green Bomber tomorrow for a shopping trip. Mom, will you run the bed-and-breakfast during our leave?"

Kate hunched her shoulders and looked at Donald. He simply said, "Yes and yes." He took his cup to the kitchen sink and rinsed it. "Come on, Kate, we need our sleep. We're not as young as we once were."

"Speak for yourself," she replied as she took short, quick steps.

Jud locked up and carried the other cups to the kitchen. Karen rinsed them out. She stopped him and placed a hand on his chest. "Jud, I'm scared. Not of planes, but about old feelings you may have about Eurlene. She's a mighty smart-looking woman. I'm not wanting to quarrel, but—"

"Darling, there is no need for you to worry your pretty little head. I love you. I need you." Stepping closer, he added, "And right now can't you tell?" He bit her earlobe. "Come lie with me?"

She put her hand in his. "Don't give me any reason to change my mind!"

He paused on the steps and brushed Karen's lips. "Are you too tired?"

The only answer he received was a hard squeeze and a pull.

Mariah spoke with Louise and Sam about taking Miechael to her mother's home in Idaho. There he could spend time getting to know them while she was in Spain.

She said, "I want Miechael to have a better opportunity knowing my parents than I had at any time."

Sam newlywed to Louise, Sara's mother, touched her shoulder and said,. "Miechael wouldn't be any trouble staying with us, but we understand and respected your decision. Mariah after all, you're the parent."

Mariah nodded and left the room. She picked up the phone and dialed. The phone rang. "Mother, hello, it's Mariah. I've been asked to attend a wedding in Spain. I was wondering if Miechael and I could come there this next week and work through some issues. And perhaps Miechael could stay with you and his grandfather for a few weeks? I don't think necessarily any longer. I will get him upon my return. Is it all right?"

"Wait a minute, Mariah. Let me get your father."

Mariah heard a click. "There, now. You're on speakerphone."

"Hello, Father."

"Mariah, your mother has filled me in. When can you bring the boy? Seeing you both will bring me happiness."

"Father, Mother, I need to let you know that the Grand Ma Mere and Duke will come there. They want to take Miechael away to boarding school, but I've decided to let Miechael stay with Ken and Sara this season and go to public school." She let out a sigh. "It's a long story. My suite at the hotel will be completed by then, and my work will be stable. Then Miechael will attend boarding school during his last three years, but on holidays, he will be home with me or I will be there with him. I'm learning that family is important."

Her mother spoke softly. "Your father and I have and can face anything or anybody. We will pray for understanding and them being supportive of your decision. When will you and Miechael be here?"

"Soon, Mother. And thanks." Mariah hung up the phone. She asked to see Miechael in her room.

"I don't want to go. You go, Mother. I'm staying here."

"Don't speak to me in that manner. Now pack! You will stay with my mother and father for three weeks. As you know, I have agreed with your stay and schooling here with Uncle Ken and Aunt Sara for this school season. I will not tolerate anyone's interference. Our hotel suite will be completed by next year, and you'll come stay with me before boarding school as we planned."

"Mother, why do I have to go?"

"I want you to get better acquainted with your grandparents, and they are pleased to have you come. You know a lot already about a farm, and they also live on one. Son, you will be a wonderful help to them. What do you say, sport?" She ruffled his hair before placing a hat on his head.

"Can I take my boots, hat, and jeans?"

"Yes, you may. Along with socks, underpants, sleepers, and one suit for church. Want me to help pack?"

"Ah, Mother."

Mariah left the room and walked out to the barn, where she spotted Ken. She waved and sat on the straw, waiting for her brother to have a free moment. Sam also waved to her. Pitchfork in hand, Ken wandered over. He picked up a piece of straw and placed it between his teeth. He tipped his hat back. "What's bothering you, Mariah? I can smell trouble."

"Stop making fun of me." Mariah stood and punched him in the arm.

"Mariah, I was teasing you. Quit. Come on now. That hurts. Don't pull the hair on my arms."

"Or what?" She nodded.

Ken forked into the straw and threatened to toss the straw on her. She said, "You know I'm in a skirt."

Ken arched his brows. "And."

Mariah tried to run. Ken caught up with her and they both bent over laughing. She was surprised how relaxed she had become around her brother.

"Ken, listen to me. I've made a decision. Miechael is going with me to Mother and Father's for a visit. He will stay there while I'm in Spain. Here are the papers I signed and had notarized for him to be in your care during the school season. Remember this is only temporary."

He placed a hand on her shoulder. "Mariah, I know this is hard. Trust doesn't come easy. I love you, and I only want the best for you and your son. It is only temporary. I think giving Mom and Dad a chance to know you and him better is the way it should be. Will you catch your flight to Spain from there?"

"I'll double-check." She reached into her file. "I'm scheduled on a flight that hooks up with J. J."

"Mariah." Ken shuffled from one foot to another.

"What?"

"I think you should give J. J. some thought."

"You don't have to worry, Ken."

"No, Mariah, you don't understand. I want you to see if you could find interest in him. He's great with the kids, and Miechael has taken a real shine to him. Yes, I know he can be an impulsive person, but he's also a solid, honest man. J. J. lost his parents at a very early age, and his sister chose to raise him. He has some education from abroad, and he is a caring person. Mariah, I want you to know that he's in love with you. We've spoken."

Mariah gasped and flung her hands to her ears. "I didn't see that coming. Ken, I don't think it could work out with J. J. He's so different and so immature." Mariah went pale and continued in a whisper. "J. J. isn't anything like Miechael's real father."

"Just pray about it. He's a God-fearing man, and he would treat you and your son right. Or he would answer to me."

She shook her head. "I just don't know." A tear formed and slowly slid down her face.

8

Mariah let out a sigh and gave Lady Ma Mere a call. "Hello. It's me, Mariah."

"Is all well, my dear?"

"Yes. I wanted to inform you that Miechael and I are staying at Mother's this week."

"What?" A long, uncomfortable silence fell. "Mariah, what on earth?"

"Grand Ma Mere, I've been staying at my brother's place, and it is good. And I intend for my son to know his grandparents better. So you know, Miechael will be attending public school from my brother's place this year."

"That is not acceptable. We'll fly in and take him abroad to continue his schooling."

"Stop this!" Mariah squealed. She willed herself to be calm. "Lady Ma Mere, I wish to thank you for all your help and care all these years. I love seeing and hearing from you, but Miechael is my child. I am going to raise him as I see fit. You don't have to agree, but I wish you would." Mariah's spine stiffened. "You see, my mother is your daughter, and I want each of us to find one another and for them to know my wonderful son. I want us to be a family."

"Don't raise your voice at me, young lady! I'm going to Sylvia's home, and we'll talk some sense into all of you."

"Grand Ma Mere?" She was gone.

Help!

Mariah's temper flared. She was in a foul mood. She called the airport immediately and arranged for her and Miechael's flight to Idaho. She was placed on hold. Her nails drummed the desk. She shifted her feet. "Come on, come on," she breathed. Finally, a man came on line, and their flight was made for later that day.

Mariah packed lightly and oversaw Miechael's. She hugged Ken, Sara, Louise, Sam, Matthew, and Timmy. She had her son change his clothes to a three-piece suit. Mariah pointed a finger. "Miechael, there's a time and place to wear cowboy duds. Correct, Ken?"

Ken put his hand on Miechael's shoulder and agreed with Mariah. "Look how I dress when I go to the bank. Image and integrity is what one builds life upon. Now hurry, Miechael."

They hugged again and got into the cab. "See you soon." They waved until they were no longer in view.

There was no delay or wait for the flight. They rested and held hands. Mariah thought, *Holding hands is new, but it brings me joy. My, how he's growing up.*

"Hi, Grandpa, Grandma."

Jon looked and nodded over at Mariah. "Miechael, you have grown. Let me have a look at you."

"Oh, Grandpa."

Sylvia asked, "Anyone hungry?"

Their ride to the ranch was merely polite. It seemed awkward to Mariah. She pressed on her skirt and fidgeted in the seat. She was glad when they turned into her parents' driveway. "It's beautiful land, Jon."

"Please try to call me Dad." He gave her a slight hug and smiled. "I'm glad you came. I really am."

"Mother, I'm tired. Will you show me to my room?" Over her shoulder, she added, "Has the Grand Ma Mere called? They are coming."

Sylvia patted Mariah's back. "We're ready for them. Your father's protective button has alarmed." She laughed. "Here's your room. Try to rest. I'll bring a tray in later." Sylvia patted her again and placed a warm kiss on Mariah's cheek.

She found a tray sitting outside her door. The hot tea was good. The toast was served with butter and orange jam. Mariah showered and stepped into a sheath dress and nine-inch heels. She pinched her cheeks for a little color, swiped on her red lipstick, and clicked her way into the kitchen.

"Hello, Mariah. It's so nice you could join us. I was speaking to Jon and Sylvia how we will take Miechael back with us and enroll him in the same school overseas that you attended."

Miechael screamed, "Mother."

Mariah held a hand up and fixed her eyes on the Grand Ma Mere then turned and watched her father. Miechael had moist, red-rimmed eyes.

Mariah adjusted her shoulders. "Miechael, did you see Jon, um, your grandfather's new tractor? I suggest you do that now! Be careful."

The door shut and Mariah began. "I'm not in fear of you." She inhaled deeply and stepped toward her grandparents. "Miechael is not going anywhere, not now or ever, with you if you don't come to your senses, Lady and Duke Ma Mere."

Grand Ma Mere seemed to tower over Mariah as she stepped and closed in on her.

Jon cleared his throat. "Let's sit down. Duke and Lady Ma Mere, it is always nice to have company. I'm sorry if you came all the way here with the wrong perception about Miechael. He will be staying with us, his grandparents, until Mariah returns from

Spain. I know you have only his best interests in mind. However, that's not traveling abroad this year to attend school." He took Sylvia's hand. "We, Sylvia and I, happen to be in agreement with Mariah and on the importance of knowing family. Unfortunately, Duke and Lady Ma Mere, you've always given orders or offered your money to intimidate instead of offering your love."

Jon rose and poured tea to those whose cups were turned upward and then he poured tea for himself. Raising a hand to stop the Mere's interference, he said, "It took me a long time to apologize to Mariah for not talking a stand with her mother against you the Ma Mere's and have Mariah summoned home when she was young and then when she was shipped abroad and esepecally after her schooling. We should have made visits. Mariah is family."

He paced the floor. "Since Sylvia turned out so well with her schooling and upbringing, all I ever wanted for Mariah was to have a great education and a love for people. So unfortunately, I let you, the grandparents, interfere. I'm sorry I didn't meet with all of you sooner to clear this stringent air." His hand was fisted, and he hit the table. "I do not, nor will I, let Miechael be persuaded by money or prestige to give up family or their values. Now let's take a walk around the farm and regroup for a calm discussion later." Standing behind Jon, Sylvia offered a hand to Mariah. "Come."

Lady Ma Mere posed with hands on the back of her chair. "Listen here. We didn't come this far to the outskirts of nowhere to be insulted."

Duke Ma Mere stood. He held out his hand to the lady. His dark brown eyes were twinkling. "You heard, Donald, my love, let's take a stroll. Is dinner at any certain time?"

Lady Ma Mere placed her hand over her heart. Moments later said, "A stroll will be nice."

Mariah awkwardly helped peel potatoes with her mother for dinner. "Mother, can you feel love? I think I did have that kind of love with my professor, and for the record, we were married."

"Mariah, God gave his only Son because of love and for us to be saved. He didn't want any person to be condemned. That is called 'agape love.' It means laying down your life for a neighbor." Stirring the fried apples, she continued. "Your father has a true, deep love. He would give his life for you or Miechael. He loved me so much before we got married, and he has abided with me unconditionally. I owe him so much."

Both had moist eyes. Mariah began mixing the meat and ingredients for meat loaf. She tilted her head and asked, "Mother, is it wrong for me to think about another man again? Is it immoral?"

Sylvia wiped her hands. "No, my dear, it is not wrong for you to think or even date another gentleman. My advice is to always pray to know God's will. He cares, and He answers."

Mariah shuffled her feet, "What temperature do I set the oven?" She watched as her mother gracefully turned the dial and opened the oven door. Her mother continued with the salad and placed it in the refrigerator.

Sylvia glanced at Mariah. "Stir the green beans and turn the heat on a simmer. Let's go outside and swing."

Jon joined Sylvia and Mariah, saying, "Miechael is showing the Ma Meres the potato field. He thinks the way potatoes are quartered and planted in their mounts and adding manure is fascinating." He looked at the women. "Am I interrupting?"

"No, Father." Mariah twisted her hands and then continued. "I've never been more proud of you than today." "You stood up for me. I feel so loved."

Sylvia fluffed her hanky, and Jon sat quietly. Almost an hour passed, and the ladies hurried to set the dinner table. The country table seated all, and the conversation began to flowed.. Shoving from the table, the duke informed Sylvia, "I can't remember when I've had a tastier meal."

"Thank you, Father. Mariah helped me."

He twisted his mustache. "Father sounds good." The duke looked at Miechael. "Son, I understand how we can be more family-oriented, but I don't want you to forget your great-grandparents' roots or their history. Being from royalty has its benefits."

"Yes, sir, I understand." He looked up. "Grand Ma Mere, I love you." He was moved to give her a squeeze.

Sylvia glanced at her mother and saw a hanky come from her sleeve. Jon stood up and stated, "We're celebrating the Christmas holidays this year at Ken and Sara's home. Arrangements have already been made." He cupped the duke's shoulder and asked, "Duke, Lady Ma Mere, why not join us this year? It would be nice. Just think about it. No need for an answer now."

"I want to thank you for your hospitality, Jon, for letting us come and express our thoughts." The duke and lady turned. "Mariah, we understand your reasoning about young Miechael's schooling. If you want or need anything, you have our number. Call us."

"Miechael"—the duke stroked the lad's dark hair—"you do well and maybe we will see you at Christmas." He approached his daughter and touched her cheek. "Sylvia, you're not only fair and beautiful, but you are wonderful and sweet. I'm proud of you and the woman, wife, and mother you have become." He bent and lightly kissed her forehead. "Come, my dear. Our plane won't wait even for us royalties."

He winked at Jon. The duke was still chuckling as he stepped into the cab.

Mariah was glad for the time she spent with her son, father, and mother, but she definitely knew that farm living was not for her. She let out a held breath when her flight was high in the heavens and the clouds looked touchable. She rested her head and closed her eyes for the journey. Her destination was quite a distance.

The server in first class asked, "Would you care for a magazine?"

She nodded and said, "Lime water please, before the meal is served." She rang for the removal of the tray, and then she lifted up and stretched her legs.

She reapplied her lipstick and face powder then smiled at her professional image staring back. Mariah leveled her hat, adjusted the veil, and stroked the plume before returning to her seat. The seat belt snapped.

Mariah licked her lips in the anticipation of landing. She delighted in seeing the skyline of Spain. She wiped the window, hoping for a better view. Mariah checked her watch and tossed her head. It was on the verge of dusk where little light appeared from the city below. But then there were the tall skyscrapers. She clutched her throat for the skyline was breathtaking.

Mariah buttoned the top of her jacket and unbuckled the seat belt. She slid on her gloves, thinking, *It will be only a matter of minutes until Eurlene greets me.* She further thought, *Shopping and more shopping—the city is full of its nightlife.* She inhaled and slowly exhaled. *Yes, this is my kind of living.*

She clutched her purse and slithered down the steps. When she walked toward the baggage claim area as instructed, the photographers called out, "It's Mariah News. Are the Ma Meres with you."

But Mariah only struck a posed for the camera and smiled. Then she gathered her luggage and waited for Eurlene.

She jumped when someone tapped her on the shoulder. Turning, she saw *him.* In a high-pitched voice, she asked, "J. J., what are you doing here? Where's your sister, Eurlene?"

J. J. reached for her luggage. "Follow me. We're walking. Do you need to change shoes?"

"What? No, I'm fine. Go on. Move."

He stood there grinning like a Cheshire cat. "All right. You hungry? We can get something."

Mariah lips scrunched. She softly spoke, "Yes, I would like to eat." She pointed out a restaurant along the square. People were sitting outside, not seeming to notice the chill in the air.

"Would you like to dine inside or out, Mariah?"

"Outside would be nice." She felt a wave come over her and felt the outside would be safer. She didn't know why she felt hot.

J. J. was the perfect gentleman. She knew he was educated in the arts because of Ken's conversation with her. J. J. asked, "May I escort you one afternoon to an art show? I picked up a schedule."

"Thank you. However, I'm not sure of Eurlene's schedule, and there's a lot that needs to be done. Let's head toward Eurlene's now."

J. J. sighed. His blue eyes lowered as they walked.

The hotel had a whitewash effect. Every row looked like snow. They were only a few steps away from where they would stay. She noticed the heavy-looking and depressing fabric of the window coverings. Stepping inside, fruits, almonds, and olives sat among the filtered tables. She ordered a salad with soup and drank iced tea. He had the same. Small talk was made. It was mostly about Spain's weather.

Later, Spencer and Eurlene arrived and joined J. J. and Mariah. They strolled through the foyer and heard someone in the crowd speak of the coming bullfight, scheduled at the festival of San Fermín. The men swore as to which matador would win. There was talk about a bull that had been chosen to be turned loose and run the streets of Pamploria, making the people flee.

J. J. nudged Spencer. "Are you and my sister planning on attending the bullfight?"

"No. I would like to though, but Eurlene feels that it's too cruel to watch the bull be speared."

Eurlene took Spencer's arm and batted her blue eyes. "Why don't you fly and take J. J. to the fight? Mariah and I will find something to entertain us here." Her lips turned upward as she patted Spencer's arm.

Spencer raised an eyebrow and bent to kiss Eurlene. They walked a little further. "J. J., would you like to see the spectacle of the bullfight?"

"Sis, is it all right with you?"

"Joshua, I didn't ask you. Spencer did." Eurlene unhanded herself from Spencer and stepped toward Mariah. "I thought we girls could go shopping for my dress. I don't want Spencer to see it."

"Eurlene, how fun. I know you will feel beside yourself when we find the right wedding dress. What time do you want to begin looking?"

"Mariah, we'll make a day of it. We will have a fruit breakfast at nine and then shop. I have a few ideas."

"Great, Eurlene. Tonight I'll make a list of your needs, and we can go over it at breakfast. I'm sorry, Eurlene. I'm a little tired tonight. I'd like to retire for the evening." She walked to the counter to retrieve a key. She held her breath when J. J. grazed her shoulder.

In a husky voice, he said, "Eurlene asked me to walk you to your room, Mariah."

She shrugged off his hand. "I don't need your help."

"Sorry. I'm headed to my room, and it's next to yours. Ken also wants you safe. He said not to take any chances—you being royalty and all."

"What?"

J. J. walked behind her and pushed the button for the elevator. She smirked. "I'm taking the stairway."

J. J. mumbled, "She's royalty all right. More like a royal pain."

"I heard that."

"And?"

"Grow up, J. J."

"Me."

They reached the top area where their suites were. "Mariah, your key please? I'll check your room for safety."

Mariah slammed the key in his hand. "Well, what are you doing in there?" She was tired and sleepy, and she was trying not to pout.

J. J. came to the living room and gave her the key. He raised his hand and pointed. "I'm next door. You can unlock the joining door if you need me."

Mariah gave him a quick look. He had a quizzical sparkle in his unforgettable blue eyes. Her stomach fluttered.

"Stop looking at me and get out. I won't be unlocking the joining door. The nerve. Go. Get out." She followed him until he stepped out the door. He turned, and their lips met. She backed away.

The vibration, which came from the door, sounded throughout the corridor.

"I only wanted to ask a question, Mariah. I didn't know you were that close." But his explanation was lost in the air.

The soaking bath did nothing to aid her sleep. In the morning, Mariah heard a ding at the door. She peeked through the opening. It was the bellhop. As she was already dressed, she opened the door and was handed a bouquet of mixed roses and daisies. Mariah tipped the bellhop and closed the door.

She smiled, stomped, and hunted for a vase. She found a tall glass and used it. She read the note.

> Sorry if I stepped out of line. You were near and, I must say, sweet. Please don't be offended. Yours, J. J.

She said, "Ken said he had changed." She let out a sigh. "J. J. is exciting but dangerous. He's different from my professor." She reached for her suit jacket and purse, locked the door, and rode down the elevator. She was still shaky.

9

"Hello, Eurlene. You look ravishing."

"I would attempt a blush, Mariah, but I've practiced my style for years. Thanks, though. Looks and business is where I am certainly self-confident. I studied abroad."

Mariah nodded. "I'm very assured with my life except…Well, let's not focus on me. It's all about you."

At the table, the ladies did brainstorming for the bride-to-be's needs. With list in hand, they passed by shop after shop that were showcasing wedding gowns. Eurlene waved her hand in the air. "These dresses are dated and not a single look of flattery."

"See!" Mariah pointed. "It's behind the front mannequin."

They stepped inside and looked. The storefront was narrow and long. The lighting was dim, and the place seemed dreary. There was a sign stating to come to the back area. There appeared to be a fashion show of wedding gowns and bridal dresses.

Eurlene checked the time, hunched her shoulders, and slithered forward. Mariah did some self-adjusting and followed. They shuffled and moved to the front seats, took an order form, and were seated. They were offered a glass of red wine or iced tea. The show began.

The first wedding dress was cute, but it could be worn at almost any dinner party. The second ballooned so much at the bottom that it was ridiculous. The third model waltzed slowly down the walk area. Eurlene began clapping, and so did Mariah, but no one else joined. The men stared down their noses, and the clerks gasped.

Eurlene stood up and demanded to see the designer. Mariah joined Eurlene. She heard Eurlene say, "Not acceptable. I'm getting married in two and a half weeks, not in six months." She pointed a finger and said, "I'll take the worn demo. You do alterations, yes?"

The man in a structured suit with a hand in his suit pocket smoothed the front of his shirt collar and loosened his tie and one button. He used a different dialect of Spanish than she was accustomed to. His face puffed as he shouted, "No!"

Eurlene's eyes flared. Mariah reached over and patted the designer on his arm. "Sir, my grandmother is the Lady Ma Mere. Shall I call her?"

Eurlene let out a long breath and fluffed her fiery hair.

"Come, ladies, to the office. I'm sure we can work out an arrangement." His lips went thin and were flat as he spoke.

Eurlene took Mariah's arm, and her brows were arched to her hairline. She began with a smile and broke into a chuckle. Eurlene waited to be seated and sat on the edge of an antique sofa. Mariah folded beside her. "Now what exactly, miss, did you like about the wedding dress you are inquiring about?" He tapped his notepad.

Eurlene licked her red lips and said, "I adore the rose appliqué on the one shoulder. And the plunging front is breathtaking. Just look at the rustic old tooling and added needle lace over the silk. It appears to be form-fitting, and I like the length."

When the veil with the woven rose design was added, they saw the way it flowed. "I pictured myself wearing that wedding dress. What more is there to say than I want it?"

The man looked at Mariah then cleared his throat. "Is your name Miss Eurlene Brown? Yes?"

Eurlene said, "My last name is Brown, soon-to-be Spencer."

His face reddening, the designer sputtered, "I have a wedding dress with me, never worn, and very similar to the one you've selected—only it is not white. It has a coffee-stain appearance, woven, and a little dusty blue ribbon at the rose area. Everything else is the same. The silk also is with the needle lace. Would you be interested in seeing it?"

Eurlene glanced at Mariah and nodded yes. Mariah scooted into the seat. The man disappeared, and they waited and waited. Eurlene said, "Mariah, make the call to your grandmother. Here is the designer's name."

Mariah patted Eurlene's arm. "Let's wait another half hour before I call. I'm sure he needed to unpack the dress or maybe he was stopped by another client."

A lady clerk stepped into the office. "Mr. Monger will be right with you. He asked me to serve you a glass of wine or perhaps tea?"

Eurlene stood and wheeled. "I'm bored." She gathered her clutch and moved from the room. "Mariah, I don't need to wait. Coming?"

Just then she heard, "Madam, here's the dress." She turned, expecting an off-brown faded something, but her breath caught. "It's almost black. Wow."

Mariah fingered the material. "Eurlene this dress is awesome."

"I'll try it on. Excuse me. Mariah, please help me."

"How's the fit, Eurlene?" Mariah handed her a veil.

"I can move inside the dress. Mariah, I'm ready to step out with the veil. What do you think?"

"From here, it looks like your second skin. The veil is a perfect match. What's not to like?"

"What's the price?"

"For you, my dear, five thousand American dollars, inclusive of the veil. You are beautiful. I could marry you myself."

Mariah coughed.

"I'll take it with me. How many euro? Thank you for accommodating my need."

His smile broadened. He held out his hand and said, "Only American money. Thank you. Is that all I can do for you?"

"Do you carry shoes?"

"Here, my lady. She can help you now." He bent and kissed Eurlene's hand.

Mariah carried the wedding dress and veil. It was heavy. Eurlene tried on at least fifty pairs of shoes before Mariah heard the wonderful words. "I'll take these and those and this and that."

They walked only a brief way when Eurlene halted. "Mariah, do you like this dress?"

"I really do. Let's try it on? It's so shockingly red. Eurlene, what do you think?"

"I love the dropped waist and the snug bodice. It's very appealing to the eyes. The jewel neckline with the cutout back is interesting and daring. You up to it?"

Mariah put her finger to her head. *Tap, tap, tap.* "Yes this is perfect. Look, there is a forest green and a bold blue dress. They are similar. Eurlene, would you want me to wear a different color?"

Eurlene looked the dresses over very carefully. "Mariah, try on the mesmerizing blue one, please."

Mariah smiled at her reflection. The silk sheath dress was made for her. Her eyes widened. The lace had baby rosebuds interspersed throughout. Mariah squealed. "Do you like it, Eurlene? It's bold."

Eurlene nudged Mariah. "Dare to be daring, little one. You're fabulous. My little brother won't know what hit him."

Mariah's blush rose from her neck to her face. "Honestly I'm not trying to reel in your brother. I admit we have some sort of an attraction, but not anything valuable or lasting. So I'm steering clear of him."

Eurlene muttered. "Right. Like you're really going to turn down J. J. when he proposes."

"What?" Mariah started shaking uncontrollably.

Eurlene made the purchase and sprung for the splashy blue matching shoes and sequined veil. Mariah purchased the undergarments to match and a beautiful gown set in red for Eurlene's wedding night. She also included nylons.

They stopped to eat and discussed what else Eurlene needed for the big day. The wedding planner Mariah obtained met with them and showed them pictures of venues to rent. The suggested table settings were in silver. The tables were round and draped in lace. Candelabra were shown in different heights with added royal blue candles. The flowers were daisies in a red-and-yellow mix, which softened the severity of the arrangement.

Eurlene was ecstatic. "Will the church have the same flowers? What about the bouquets and boutonnieres?"

"Relax, senorita. Here are the photos of the flower arrangements made especially for you to wear. These are the vases shown filled with the same grouping of flowers for the church. You like it?"

Mariah felt shuffled from pillar to post in helping Eurlene get ready for the wedding.

The next night Ken, Sara, Jud, and Karen were due.

J. J. was helpful and polite, but he kept his distance. Eurlene requested Mariah to go on a daytime date with J. J. and see the Circle of Fine Arts while they were in Madrid. They left the hotel at 9:00 a.m. They were scheduled to see the artist's sketch. They were seated along with many others, and they enjoyed the artist's specialty work. Mariah's mind drifted to the dark past about her artist professor. She saw him clear as day, stroking an image of her with his brush as he was worked. She dabbed her eyes, which threatened to fill with tears.

J. J. placed an arm around her and patted her shoulder. "You want to leave? Come, let's walk around. I'm sorry this brought hurtful memories back. I had hoped for us to have an airy, happy day."

Mariah leaned over to J. J. and surprisingly placed her head on his shoulder. "I'm all right now. Thanks for understanding."

They watched the artist for another hour then left and went gallery hopping. Mariah stopped short. "Look, J. J., the people in the picture remind me of us, but why are they standing in a wheat field instead of under city lights?"

He laughed. "Mariah, that's modern art, and it's not a wheat field. It's a fence row." He took her hand and guided her to an outside café. "Would you like a hot tea?"

"Yes." Mariah looked around. "J. J., watch the people and tell me a story about them. Then I'll tell you a story."

Time rolled into evening. They strolled down the street and looked into windows and told many stories. Along the way, they found a fountain. J. J. handed Mariah a coin to toss in, and he did likewise. "Did you make a wish, Mariah?"

She nodded with a slight smile. They finally met up with Eurlene and Spencer. The four went to dinner and took in a show.

J. J. asked. "Sis, are you nervous about tomorrow?"

She tossed her head, and her fiery curls bounced. "Hmm, no, I'm not nervous. But I'm truly thinking about the responsibilities of marriage and its confinement."

Spencer, sitting nonchalantly, jerked his head and stared directly into her blue-green eyes. He calmly stated, "Well, my love, if you are not sure about me and the ultimate way I feel about you, then I won't see you at the altar." He closed his arms around her and kissed her hard. Spencer lifted his face and said, "J. J., see that Eurlene gets to her suite. I need to make a few calls. Excuse me, ladies." He smiled as he put his hands into his trouser pockets and walked away, leaving no doubt to anyone that he was all man.

"Sis, what were you thinking? He's a great man. Honest and God-fearing. He's withheld nothing from you. He has offered you his life, his home, and his money without any prenuptials.

Not to mention that he's extremely handsome. He's a catch many women have tried to land. I just don't get women."

Mariah watched Spencer walked away. She turned to Eurlene, but her eyes were glassy. No words were spoken. The walk back to the hotel was cold and lonely. Mariah offered to see herself to the hotel room, but Eurlene held up a hand. "We're here, J. J. I have a stop in the hotel to make. I don't intend on you watching out for me. Not now, not ever. Take care of Mariah. Just go!"

J. J. took Mariah's arm a little harder than was necessary and escorted her upstairs. She struggled, but he stood firm and stared as Mariah placed the key into the door's slot and watched the door open. Mariah looked over her shoulder and then turned.

Mariah surprisingly smiled. "J. J., thanks for being my companion today. For the most part, I had a great time." She stood on tiptoe and kissed his cheek. He was warm and manly. His eyes turned the color of steel. "J. J., would you like to come in?"

He was reluctant to step across the threshold, and his eyebrows were raised. Mariah's smile deepened as she reached for his lapel and pulled him into the room.

"Do you know what you're doing, Mariah? My feelings run deep for you. I'm not someone to add to your collection of leftovers. I've hit it off with your boy, and we have become close. Mariah, I love you and your son. I've never told anyone that before, except for my sister, but not in the same way of course. Oh, you know what I mean." J. J. ran a hand through his red hair.

Mariah wrapped her arms around his waist and saw his blue eyes change from indecisive to soft. She stretched up to kiss him for he didn't bend. She moved her hand into his thick, wavy red hair and pulled his face down to hers. She whispered, "J. J., trust in people is not easy. Things have happened in my life, and change is hard."

Mariah slid her hands down to her sides. "I do have feelings for you, J. J. I would be lying if I said differently. Although I'm not interested in having a physical relationship with you or any other man. But a lasting union, the way God intends for a man and woman to be, I might someday consider." Mariah tipped her head back. "I do like being wooed." She smiled, and it reached her hazel eyes.

J. J.'s eyes widened. "I would like for us to continue our talk, perhaps in more detail, but right now I must see to Eurlene. I wouldn't want to be on Spencer's blacklist." J. J. turned then paused. "May I see you tomorrow after we adjourn from the crowd coming in for Spencer and Eurlene's wedding?"

Biting her trembling lip, Mariah said, "J. J., if there is to be a possible 'us,' we need to take things slow. I don't need demands or pressures on either one of us." Mariah clasped her hands and waited. She hoped for a kiss, but he nodded, smiled, then proceeded to the door, and said, "Bolt this door now."

As she leaned against the door, Mariah said, "I'm in conflict with myself, Lord. I'm scared of gaining and losing again like in my horrible past." The tears fell. She willed herself to shower. She hoped to find rest as she lay on the bed. But in the next few hours, she tossed, turned, and rolled over. Mariah finally reached for a picture of her professor and brought it close to her heart. Feelings of fear and confusing were creeping. She rubbed her eyes, and sleep drifted in.

10

Eurlene held on to Spencer, a confident man. He appeared so powerful but relaxed as the groom-to-be. He swaggered as he strutted toward their guests. She waved, and Jud and Ken waved back. Eurlene hugged Karen and then Sara. She said, "Thank you both for coming. I know schedules are hard to adjust, but ladies, I'm worth it."

She walked over to Jud, pulled him into a hug, and kissed him on the cheek. She then grabbed Ken. He swung her around. "Hello, men, I'm present."

Spencer chuckled. He walked over to the men, and said, "She's taken."

They shook hands, and each man offered him congratulations. Jud whispered, "Old boy, you've got your hands full for the rest of your life."

Spencer's lips were pursed. "I'm up for the challenge. Why do you think she accepted my proposal?"

J. J. joined Spencer, Ken, and Jud. He said, "Men, we have a full day planned."

Eurlene spoke up. "It's party time, ladies. Mariah, Karen, and Sara, let's walk around, enjoy the sights, and shop." They all had massages, pedicures, and nail enhancements. They felt like rubber. It was nice talking with each other and catching up on the news about the new lambs, fencing, and the horses. While the ladies were together, Karen and Sara sprang their news about being pregnant.

Suddenly, Karen felt ill. She said, "I should only drink boiled water." Covering her mouth, she said, "Eurlene, Mariah, Sara, I'm going to the suite to lie down. I need to let my stomach settle. What time do you want us to meet up for the wedding, Eurlene?"

Eurlene thumbed through her agenda book. "We'll have a light breakfast at 9:00 a.m. and then catch the flight to Marbella. Our hair appointments are scheduled at 11:30 a.m. Rooms are booked at the hotel, and after a rest, we'll meet at the church by 2:00 p.m. The wedding is at 2:30 p.m. Call down and order anything. It's on me. And hot tea and crackers might help. Us girls—myself, Sara, and Mariah—will continue shopping. Hope you feel better, Karen."

Karen gave a quivering smile, waved, and rode the elevator. The uneasiness passed as she neared the suite's door. Jud stood in the doorway. "Well, Mrs. Day, what would you like to do?"

"Honestly, change into comfy clothes and flop in bed." She raised an eyebrow. "Maybe read."

"Karen, I'll draw you a bubble bath. Would you like me to leave oils and salts by the tub's side? Take your time. I'll order in for us."

She patted his chest. He gasped. She glanced at his green eyes, and they deepened. She edged into the tub where the bubbles were whirling. Yellow rose petals rested on top. She breathed in the aromas. After an hour, she dried and splashed on new perfume.

Jud was leaning on one hand and reading in bed. His shirt was slightly unbuttoned, and he was barefoot. He looked relaxed. With a youthful grin, he said, "Here, Karen, slide in. They're silk sheets. Don't fall." He stood up and said over his shoulder, "I'll be right out."

The shower ran, and she could hear him singing. It had been a long time hearing his voice. She fluffed her pillows then answered the door to the bellhop. She gave him the tip Jud had left out. She unfolded in a straight-backed chair and poured herself and Jud cups of tea. She heard a noise and looked up. Jud was standing in his pajamas.

"I stubbed my toe. Want to kiss it?"

"Jud, come get your tea." She winked. Untying her robe, she said, "Jud, dim the lights. I have something to tell you."

Sara, Mariah, and Ken stayed together after Spencer, Eurlene, and a reluctant J. J. retired to their rooms.

"Mariah," Ken softly spoke. "Want to talk about J. J.?"

"No. Not really. I'm still processing facts about him, but thanks for the offer."

"How are you and Eurlene getting along?"

"Ken, Sara, underneath all that makeup and stiffness, she is very sweet and nice. Although she doesn't let her guard down much. We did butt heads in the beginning, but now we've agreed to disagree." Mariah smiled. "Sara, how was the flight?"

"Well, having your brother to cling to, I'm all right."

Ken rubbed his arm and laughed.

"Sara, I hope you like the dress we picked out for you to wear for the wedding. It's yellow. And Sara, thanks for the letter you left in my suitcase."

Ken turned with an arched brow.

Sara shifted a little. "Mariah, I want us to be close. Perhaps after we return home you could stay for a visit?"

Mariah kissed Sara on the cheek and then Ken, and she said, "I won't be able this time, but I'm coming in for Christmas break." She yawned. "I think it's time I turn in. Tomorrow is the big day."

"Wait up, sis. We'll ride with you and see you to your room."

Arm-in-arm, they joked and laughed and took the elevator. Mariah opened her door and kissed her brother on the cheek. She watched him turn and walk back onto the elevator. Mariah closed the door and switched on a light.

Mariah whispered, "Is someone in here?" She slowly walked toward the sofa. "It's Joshua, and he's asleep."

Ken smiled as he walked Sara to their room. He knelt down and slipped off her shoes and helped remove the nylons. Then he began massaging her feet. Sara pulled her foot and giggled from the thumb movement he did around her toes. "Thanks, Ken. My feet feel much better." She picked up her nightgown and padded to the bathroom. "I'll be right out."

He smiled as he heard the shower. He checked his clothes he was wearing for the wedding. He picked up the cuff links and placed them on the side table by his newly shined black shoes.

Sara passed him as she sat in front of the mirror, brushing her black silken hair. He grabbed a towel and grinned. He slowly rinsed off the soap and towel dried his long black hair. He put on his pajama bottom and winked at Sara.

She led him by the hand, saying, "Let's go over our steps for tomorrow."

He turned the radio on and searched for a song. Sara switched the off button. She began singing and encouraging him. She placed her hand in his. He placed the other hand on her back, and they began to waltz. They were a good fit. They turned and swayed with the music. He tilted her back and raised her to his bent head, and their lips touched. "Umm, you taste like sweets." His darkened eyes appeared timeless. Sara gripped his hand tighter. "Come with me."

Mariah, still in her street clothes, felt cold and was shivering. She glanced around her semidark room and looked for J. J., but he was gone. She said, "How long was he in here asleep? What would my brother think of me? Especially not being married to J. J.. Ken is so old-fashion. I know there would be another wedding all right, a shotgun wedding, like it or not." She hurried and bathed, hoping she wouldn't be late in joining the others for breakfast.

Eurlene left a note at the front desk for Mariah.

> Come to the church after you eat. I mustn't see Spencer. Bring the maid of honor dress and change here. I'm to pick out music, but I really don't know what I'm doing.

Mariah folded the note and ate. Afterward, she went to the suite and gathered her special wear and the wedding clothes. She took one last check of her makeup and smiled. "Looking good."

Mariah flagged a cab. She could barely see over the clothing and things she was carrying. The load became too heavy. J. J. bumped into her and said, "Sorry. Here let me take the shoe tote or the hatbox or both."

But Mariah said, "No. Get away from me. Go find someone else to care about." She was rude. He didn't waver; he held the door open and complimented Mariah on her organization skills. He was wearing that stupid smile.

She turned to walk away, and he grabbed her arm. His pressure was unwavering. Mariah spoke. "Let go." But music was playing on the street and people were cheering to it, so her words were lost. She lifted her foot. J. J., watching her every move, sidestepped. He tipped his hat and gave her a bow.

Mariah was fuming. She tried to poke him but to no avail. He gave a wicked smile and then kissed her. She squirmed and took steps, but the kiss deepened. Her heart raced.

He reached over and relieved her of the packages. "You're beautiful, Mariah. You may steal the show. You will in my eyes, anyhow."

Mariah blushed and fumbled for words. She could only say, "Thank you for your kindness." She walked into the dressing room where Eurlene was tapping her nails on a side table. "What took you so long?"

Mariah answered, "I took a cab, and your brother appeared, offering to help me carry everything inside."

Eurlene picked up the boxes and glanced over her shoulder. "Mariah, J. J. has changed for the better. You've caught him. As a warning, don't use him and don't hurt him. Have you thought what you really want out of life? Mariah, have you even prayed? And do you have peace with your past?"

Eurlene clutched the wedding bag and soon wriggled into her dress. She smoothed it over her curvy hips.

"You're breathtaking, Eurlene. Spencer won't be able to take his eyes off you."

"Thanks. And look at you, Mariah. I think we must be the same size. Say, what shade of lipstick are you wearing?"

Mariah chuckled. "It's Kissing Red from the new line I modeled."

"Have an extra?"

Mariah opened her purse. "Eurlene, it doesn't fade nor come off. Here's a new tube."

"Thanks." Eurlene quickly applied an application, blotted, and reapplied. "My, this shade looks divine on me too, only different."

The music began, and the soloist sang. She floated from one song to another. Eurlene and Mariah prayed in the side room provided for them at the church, and then they peeked though the doorway. Eurlene saw Jud, who was truly handsome and tall and who stood beside Spencer at the front. Just for the moment, her thinking went to another time and place. *How could I have ever thought I was in love with Jud even after high school?* Eurlene giggled more to herself and whispered, "Well, he is fine-looking and those green, green eyes." Eurlene's eyes blinked and locked on her husband-to-be.

Spencer was tanned from being on holiday. When he smiled, both of his dimples showed. His hair shined; it had been freshly cut and styled. His black one-button suit didn't have a wrinkle, and it fit his body well. He was such an assured man.

Eurlene glanced and saw Karen and Sara sitting together. The fifty-some candles of random sizes were lit, and the flower arrangements were incredible as promised. She nodded to Mariah to lead the way. They walked up a dreary hall and entered the back of the church. The lady finished with the song, and the organ began. Mariah waltzed and swayed slowly to the front where the men stood. All eyes were on her. A flash came, and then another.

Mariah clutched her bouquet, not skipping a beat but not seeing too well.

Jud whispered, "Turn to the left, Mariah."

She turned and stood in place. She glanced at Jud and mouthed, "Thank you." She batted her eyes. All instruments ceased playing. Moments went by; then the wedding march was pounded out. Everyone stood up. Cameras snapped from everywhere, in all directions.

J. J. offered his arm to Eurlene. His black suit highlighted Eurlene's dress. She glanced at him and placed her hand on his arm.

J. J. smilingly said, "You're beautiful, sis." He patted her hand.

Swish, swish went the form-fitting silk dress covered in lace. The veil flowed from the top of her pinned-up hair until it touched the floor.

Someone from the crowd said, "Eurlene you're bewitching."

Eurlene slowly made exaggerated steps, and her hips swayed. Mariah watched Spencer. His darkened eyes widened with each step, and his grin deepened. He shifted his position and held out his hand, anticipating the moment that Eurlene would join him.

Eurlene turned slightly and handed Mariah her flowers as J. J. took his position next to Jud. Mariah was her maid of honor. Mariah listened to the vows, but her head felt a spin. The scent of J. J.'s aftershave wafted her way.

Within fifteen minutes, Eurlene and Spencer were pronounced man and wife. The minister said, "You may kiss the bride."

Every eye was glued to the moment of the beautiful couple. *Snap, snap, snap* went the cameras.

Spencer and Eurlene selected the perfect wedding spot, Marbella; it was exotic.

Mariah was secretly glad that the ceremony was in English, although it was with a thick accent. Bells rang, and Spencer motioned for everyone to follow them for the outdoor reception.

Lights were draped everywhere. There was a mammoth fireplace, and the grill was already in service. Spanish women weaved in and out from the tables, bringing food and drinks. An area was set aside for the Spaniards to play their guitars and accordion. Ken and Jud surprised the bride and groom and the guests by playing and singing "I Love You Truly." Every woman, young or old, swooned.

The dance area became crowded.

Eurlene danced the first dance with Spencer, and then they separated to dance with another partner. Eurlene danced with J. J., and Spencer with Mariah. Karen clapped, and so did Sara. Ken asked Sara to join him in dancing, as did Jud when he bowed in front of Karen and offered his hand.

The evening wore on until midnight. The mood was definitely of love and more. J. J. tapped Spencer on the shoulder and resumed the dance with Mariah.

She was surprised at his light footwork and flexibility. He held the lead, and his smile was deadly. He kept proper distance between them until the music changed to a slow dance. He drew her close, placing his hand on the middle of her back. Flesh to flesh. She stepped even closer. *Snap, snap, snap* went the cameras. He twirled them, and they posed. They had comfortable conversations.

The music stopped unexpectedly J. J. tilted her back. His grip was tight yet gentle. She stood, and he leaned in where their lips almost met.

Who kissed whom? Did it matter? She remembered firm, warm, supple lips taking control. J. J. smiled and stepped backwards. He bowed and offered his arm to her. She felt sad and happy. She was in a tumult, carrying so many mixed emotions. Mariah looked at him with raised eyebrows.

"Miss Day, may I court you when we arrive back in the States? I've spoken to Ken, and he's given his permission as well as your father's."

She shifted positions, stiffening.

"Darling"—he slid to one knee—"will you accept this promise ring, Mariah? I love you and Miechael."

The crowd clapped, and Ken strummed his guitar. He smiled broadly as he looked at his sister. Mariah placed her hands to her face. She was shivering as J. J. stood up and drew her nearer to him. She looked in his blue eyes and saw new hope, honesty, and love. J. J.'s sky blue eyes twinkled as she squeezed his hand. "My heart is beating trust, but I'm terrified, Joshua." She nodded then said, "I'll agree in faith. Here's my hand."

11

"Calling Mr. Day. Judwin Day."

"That's me."

"Sir, you have a phone call from Miss Phyler. Here."

"Hello, Miss Phyler? This is Jud. What's wrong?"

She seemed out of breath. "Oh, sir, what a mess." She clucked her tongue.

"Calm down, Miss Phyler. Let me know what's the matter."

"Well, Mr. Day, there are issues. The first one: Mrs. Page called and asked if I had spoken with you or Karen. Since I hadn't, here is the message: Karen's doctor needs her to come in for another physical."

"Why?"

"Hush now! I wasn't finished. The doctor said Karen might be carrying twins again."

He heard Miss Phyler tap her notepad. She continued. "Next, Jack is outside your office prancing back and forth and wearing out the carpet."

J. J. broke in. "What's wrong?"

"Who's not calm now, Mr. Day?" She cleared her throat. "He has brought Claudia back with him to the bed-and-breakfast thinking Karen would be there. Sir, Jack, they want to get married now. You know I didn't sign on for all this, Mr. Day. Mr. Day?"

He let out a held breath, "Yes, Miss Phyler."

"Sir, your return flight arrangements are made for you and the missus tonight. Your flight leaves in less than two hours."

He cleared his throat and said, "Thanks, Miss Phyler."

"Oh, Jud, Karen is to call her mother. And from me, congratulations on the pregnancy. Bye-bye."

Jud raked his hand through his rich chocolate-colored hair. "Man, Miss Phyler's voice is shrill."

Jud placed a finger around his tight-fitting collar and glanced Karen's way. She was sitting, heavy in conversation. He realized she was glowing. Jud walked toward her with new knowledge. "Karen, my love, we need to return home." Jud grinned slightly. "Jack is wearing out the carpet at the bank, and Claudia is at the bed-and-breakfast. We have a wedding to plan. They're not waiting to wed." He placed a hand on Karen's shoulder.

"Jud, we need Sara and Mariah in on this to help us." Then she smiled and giggled.

Jud offered her his hand. "Sweetheart, is there anything else you need to tell me?" His eyebrows went upward.

Karen squeezed his hand and looked into his green eyes. "I do, but later. We must let our friends in on the wedding event that will take place at home. We also need to say our good-byes. Let's get a move on it." She patted his arm. "We also need to pack and catch the plane."

Jud saluted, clicked his heels, and motioned for their friends to join them. At the gathering, Jud announced, "Karen and I are departing in a little while for the USA." He shook his head and then explained. "Jack and Claudia have changed their minds about a courtship. They want to get married at the bed-and-breakfast."

Karen held out her arms to her lady friends, Sara and Mariah. As they encircled her, she said, "You know I can't pull off this shindig without you both. We have less than a month, max. What do you say?"

Sara motioned Ken over and whispered in his ear. Karen watched and saw him laugh while nodding his head yes.

Mariah shifted from one foot to the other. "Karen, I need to pick up Miechael first and then call my agent."

J. J. stood with his hands on his hips, looking on and listening to the news of the upcoming wedding of Claudia and Jack.

Ken spoke. "Mariah, why don't you fly with Sara? Take my place. I'll stop at Mother's and get Miechael. We'll join you at Karen's." He turned with arms wide open and asked, "Karen, do you have room for all of us and your guest?"

Karen's blue eyes twinkled. "Sure. It's a surprise, but before we left, Jud and I began working with our architect. The rustic barn is now a four-level apartment complex complete with bathrooms. And there's a kitchen and laundry site on the ground. The turkey house is now a three-bedroom homey bungalow." Karen looked directly at Sara. "Girl, I need your help quick for the designs and furnishings."

Mariah began to speak, but Eurlene eased an arm around Mariah and said, "Karen, dear, Mariah can help Sara pull in favors on fashion furnishings. I'll call my people in New York and ask them to work with Mariah and Sara." She looked at Sara. "Call me with a list, and the furnishings will be shipped. So ladies, you can begin designing. Spencer and I"—she dropped her head—"will join you in one week. Spencer can help the men, and we'll make this wedding spiffy." Eurlene laughingly strolled over to Spencer.

Karen touched Mariah's chin. "We're family now and friends."

A week passed, and life was chaotic. Spencer had drawn up papers for the B and B rental/lease usage, and he gave them to Karen. Tom and his wife, Dora as well as Joan and her husband of one year, Eli, made a surprise visit to the bed-and-breakfast. Not even their son, Jud, knew they were coming. So Tom and Joan, along with their significant others, quickly got into the spirit of the upcoming country wedding. All the ladies worked together. Karen bit her lip at times to hold the peace.

Jon and Sylvia called Karen, hearing about the wedding, Jon said, "Jud and Ken may need my help in preparing the wood frame for the wedding structure."

Sylvia added, "And I'm sure you ladies will need help in baking."

Karen handed out last-minute assignments. Mariah and Eurlene were to take Claudia into town for the purchase of her wedding ensemble and nightwear for the honeymoon. Donald, with Tom and Eli, took Jack and rented the groom and groomsmen's western-style suits.

Karen, Kate, Sylvia, Joan, and Dora worked steadily on decorations in the newly erected banquet hall and the menu for Claudia and Jack's wedding celebration. The men placed bales of straw in a circular pattern, and they placed wagon wheels sporadically throughout. A chuck wagon was delivered with an overhead sign reading "Chow."

Cactus glasses were arranged to serve Karen's famous brewed iced tea. The men added bleached cow heads and horseshoes on the walls. It gave the place a real country feeling.

Karen rocked on her shoes and nervously laughed. "The only thing missing in here is some tumbleweed rolling through."

The bed-and-breakfast was filled to its capacity with family, friends, and guests. No matter what anyone's plans were, they all came together in helping with Jack and Claudia's wedding celebration. And everyone had opinions.

Sara was surprised. She was elected to making Claudia's wedding dress. Claudia had not liked anything that Eurlene and Mariah saw. Sara brought on a crew to help—her mother, Louise; Karen's mother, Kate; Ken's mother, Sylvia; and Jud's mother, Joan, as well as his stepmother, Dora.

Sara designed a wedding dress sketch, which Claudia liked. And a sign was posted over Karen's office in bold letters: "No men allowed." The ladies sounded like bumblebees. They only left their work area to eat and briefly help Karen in the kitchen.

Claudia tried on the pinned dress. She fussed and fumed and pouted and stomped her feet, but Mariah had a calming effect. Two weeks later, when Claudia tried on the final version of the white wedding dress, she cried, "Oh, look at me."

Sara stood with tape measure in hand and mouth holding straight pins. Louise held her hands, and Kate's mouth gaped. Sylvia, Joan, and Dora clapped hands.

The neckline of Claudia's dress was square. And the dress was sleeveless, but a short-capped lace jacket was added. The material was plain; the circular skirt needed three more crinolines sewn in for support. The veil was short and designed with a hint of embroidered roses. The ensemble was a quintessence of its era.

Her bouquet was small yet perfectly filled with baby yellow and white roses. Some baby's breath was added to the bouquet's fullness.

Karen did Claudia's makeup while Mariah sketched Claudia's hairstyle. Karen then brought the design to life, pinning Claudia's hair in a partial upsweep. Her dangling orange-red curls of different lengths were dazzling.

The men wore black boots, slacks, and white long-sleeve shirts, with black armbands that were touched off with chokers engraved with silver saddles. Their vests all carried the same silver emblem. Jud and Ken helped the men with their boutonnieres. Spencer was surprised but pleased when the men made him take off his coat and pinned on the silver emblem on his vest.

Jack wore white, from his cowboy hat to his cowboy boots. He added a choker, same as the men. The music started. The men took their stand and watched the ladies proceed down the stairway.

The fiddles were playing, with Jud and Ken picking and stamping out the beat. The dining hall was filled. All doors were ordered to stay open. The transformation was becoming. The railings of the stairs leading from the four unit apartments were wrapped in baby's breath and entwined with little white and yellow rose buds. Lanterns set at different heights and of all shapes and sizes were used.

Silence fell upon the audience as the ladies descended the steps wearing their powder-blue ballerina dresses. Only light music was heard in the background as well as an occasional laugh. Jud and Ken sang as Claudia, on Donald's arm, walked down the aisle. Claudia's face glowed and her features softened as she neared Jack. He stepped forward and took her hand, and in a whisper, he said, "You, my charmer, are breathtaking."

Claudia smiled and batted her eyes. She raised an arm and elbowed Jack. He moved a little and winked while squeezing her hand. Jack's knees were trembling.

The minister pronounced Jack and Claudia as husband and wife. Stepping back, he announced, "You may kiss the bride."

Hats were tossed, and the hollering began. Karen rang a cowbell, and Mariah said, "You all come and get it."

Some music was lively, but there were a few slow songs scattered in the mix. As the piano was wheeled in, the accordions purred. Jud and Ken took their moves to the dance floor as they swung Karen and Sara. The announcer for the night was J. J., and he informed the group that a bailing of us gathered together and a trip to the cottage where the newlyweds would be surprised and welcomed. The happening in the wee hours.

J. J. silenced the room as he glanced up and saw the Duke and Lady Ma Mere. Mariah rushed to them as the Duke waved J. J. on to continue. Sara, Ken, Spencer, and his overbearing wife, Eurlene, took Karen and Jud's hands and formed a circle around their new guests.

The duke sought Sylvia out and also motioned to Jon. Donald and Kate stepped forward to support their friends. Duke Ma Mere looked at Mariah then at Sylvia. "I understand today's wedding was not my granddaughter's and Joshua Brown's. Is that correct, Sylvia?"

But Karen spoke up. "Excuse me. No, it wasn't their wedding, or you would have been invited." With her hands on her hips, she rolled her blue eyes and said, "Who do you think you are busting your way in here?"

Jud touched his wife's arm and tried guiding her away. Karen refused. Instead, she asked, "Sir, Duke Ma Mere, would you have this dance with me?" And surprisingly, she gave him a curtsy.

Lady Ma Mere placed her arm on Karen's. "Woman, you are way out of line."

The duke stepped forward, bowed, and flicked his mustache. His brown eyes appeared lively. They glided on the floor and waltzed to a refined tune brought by Ken. They were the only couple twirling. Jon whisked Sylvia on the floor and in grand ease showed off a hidden talent: dancing. As Jud faced her, showing his dimple, he bowed and asked, "Ma'am, Lady Ma Mere, may I have this dance?"

She opened her eyes wider, but she gave a quick curtsy and offered her gloved hand. Jud had formal training, but was a little rusty. It took him a few dance steps, but then to the audience they whooped and called, "Bring it on, Fred Astaire and Ginger Rogers."

Jud gave a beaming smile and then was tapped on the shoulder. He bowed as he thanked Lady Ma Mere and offered her hand to the duke. Karen was radiant. Jud step forward, bowed, and whirled with Karen. They completed circling the room, and Jud offered her hand to Ken and replaced him on stage with an instrument. They stopped in front of Sara. Karen pleaded. "Take your cowboy and do-si-do."

Sara motioned for Jud to liven up the music. "Ken, this is weird, but I'm really having fun. But, oh my, poor Karen."

Ken nodded as they danced. "Baby girl, she's a wild cat. She's got everything under control."

"You think so, Cowboy?" Smiling, he arched a brow.

J. J. did the calling. A square dance was formed. Claudia led, and Jack followed. There were four groups on the floor, including the Duke and Lady Ma Mere. The dancing continued until 10:00 p.m. The new bride and groom finally disappeared, and the guests slowly dwindled.

Only the cleanup crew was left. Jud rolled up his shirtsleeves, showing his strong forearms, and began pushing a broom.

Sam motioned to Louise. He said, "Can you usher the children to the house? They are past being tired, and their beds are calling them."

Louise clapped her hands and whistled. Luke, Luci, Timmy, Matthew, and Miechael marched.

Karen flopped and then bent over, taking off her shoes. She fingered her toes. She heard a clearing of the throat and looked up. Standing there were the Ma Meres. Karen didn't bother replacing her shoes. A man, one of the guests, had out his wallet with a pile of money. He addressed Karen and said, "Thanks for such a great time. Here's the money for the misses and my stay. Do remember to schedule us at around the same time next year. We are the Terry family."

Karen held his money and said, "Follow me. I'll give you a receipt."

He flagged his hand. "Oh shucks, Karen, just mail it."

The man left as Karen said, "Be safe. See you next year." She forced a laugh as she walked over to the Ma Meres. The duke lifted his hand in jest. "Do you have any rooms available for the night, Mrs. Day?"

Lady Ma Mere turned with her mouth completely open. "Harold, were you thinking of staying in this place here tonight?"

"I'm sorry, dear. I didn't call ahead and make any reservations. I really didn't think it was necessary in this small town's area."

Karen put her fisted hands to her sides and let out a held breath. She was past exhaustion. Her legs were weak, her feet were cramped, and her face hurt to smile. Jud appeared at her side and placed an arm around her waist. "What do we have here, more guests?"

Karen muttered, "They didn't make reservations, but there's a suite available."

Jud looked at Karen sideways and with a raised brow. "Where do I carry their luggage to?"

"Suite 2-D will do nicely. Thanks, Jud." She turned to the Duke Ma Mere, saying, "If you both will follow me to the office, we can get you registered there. Lady Ma Mere, would you like a pot of hot tea sent to your room?"

"Karen, that would be wonderful indeed. Thank you."

"Please be seated on the bench, and I'll be right back to show you to your suite."

Within minutes, a light knock sounded on suite 2-D's door. "Karen?"

Jud stood outside. She grabbed his vest and halfway pulled him in.

"Help me!" With hands held out, she said, "I'll make the bed while you gather Claudia's things and take them to our room. Then I'll clean the bathroom. Come on, be quick."

"Karen, I brought our guests up. They're in the hall."

Karen left him standing, tied an apron around her, and tucked her dress in at the band. She finally lifted her head and arms from cleaning the commode. She glared at Jud and blew a puff of air from the side of her mouth. It fanned the loose hair that had now slipped down around her face. Jud closed his eyes. He knew he had done the wrong thing by having the duke and his wife upstairs. He didn't hear anything so he opened an eye.

Karen set the brush and bucket down, curtsied, and opened the door. She said, "Sir, ma'am, your suite is now available. Just ring the number at the side of the phone should you need me. Breakfast is at seven thirty tomorrow morning due to the bailing at the cottage, which is yet on today's schedule. You're welcome to come if you would like to participate." She squared her shoulders and laid a chocolate sweet on each pillow. She thrust clothing and articles in Jud's arms, nodded, and walked backward out their door. She pushed Jud out and bid the Ma Meres a good night.

"Darling."

She put a hand up and turned her head. "Just take this pot of tea upstairs to suite 2-D and place it with the cheese cracker snack on the side table outside their door and rap twice, then leave. Got it?"

Jud's lips lifted, and a smile cracked on his face. The delivery of the tea and snack was done. He tiptoed into his and Karen's bedroom. He made sure the clock was set for them to be ready for the bailing, and he muttered, "Only two and half hours to sleep." He looked in Karen's direction, and she was almost asleep. He dropped his clothes and kicked them in a corner and took a much-needed shower. He stretched then turned his head from side to side. He grabbed a huge towel and rummaged through the drawer looking for his pj's.

Karen lifted her head. "Is it time to go?"

Jud touched her hair. "No, darling, just sleep." He let out a deep, deep breath. He glanced at his hands before turning the light out; they were trembling. He slipped under the sheet and kissed Karen's forehead, whispering, "I love you so."

Karen turned and placed a hand on his chest, and it seemed to him she was smiling. The ringer on the clock sounded like an alarm. Karen jumped, and Jud reached the button and hit off, not snooze. "Let go, sleepyhead."

Karen hit him with a pillow and stood up. Jud bellowed with laughter. Karen could hear him from the kitchen.

The guests attending the bailing were waiting, but not the Ma Meres. Jud and Karen both passed out long-handled spoons, pans, and washtubs. They were all off to bid the newlyweds.

"Wait up."

Karen saw Sara and Ken running toward them. "Sara, my eyes want to close."

"I'm sure they do. My fingers hurt and are still swollen. I even have calluses on them from sewing." Before Karen could speak, Sara asked, "Where are the Ma Meres?"

"Not here, that's for sure." She snorted. "Jud helped me with Claudia's old suite and they are now staying in 2-D. Since Jack had the cabin out back, I knew Claudia and he would want to honeymoon out there. I don't know why the Ma Meres came. It's trouble I sure don't need."

Jack and Claudia came to the front door, he in plaid pajamas and matching robe and Claudia in a flannel granny gown with a cap on her head. Her robe was terry cloth. Claudia flung her arms. "What the Sam Hill are you all doing out there making all that racket?"

Jack patted her back. "It's a bailing."

"A what?"

Everyone bent over laughing. The moon was full, low, and bright. Karen saw happiness in the eyes of her parents, Jud's parents, and Ken and Sara's parents. They were holding hands or had an arm around each other. Jud began singing, and the group joined in.

Jack asked, "Hot chocolate, anyone?"

12

The sun played peekaboo through the cotton-shaped clouds, but the wind stood still and silent. Although, in the house, the fireplace crackled.

Karen hung her coat on the rack as Jud entered the room. She pointed and said, "Please pull both dining and kitchen tables together. We need the seating for the guests, family, and friends. You know, Jud, breakfast doesn't wait." She cracked the fresh brown eggs collected from the henhouse while the bacon, sausage links, and patties sizzled. A king-size loaf of bread was toasted. Karen set coffee, iced tea, brewed hot tea, homemade tomato juice, freshly squeezed orange juice, and milk on the serving counter.

She dabbed her forehead then rang the dinner bell. Everyone, both young and old, gathered around the table. Jud smiled and asked each to take hands. He prayed blessings and safety for each person.

Much chatter encircled the table. Different ones spoke of their departures. Karen motioned the people to leave the table setting, for she would clean up after good-byes were said. She hugged her mother and father, and Jud gave his endearments. The Ma Meres entered the room. The duke caught Donald by his coat cuff. "Wait up, ole boy. We've decided to come along with you on the Bahamas cruise. We called the cruise line, and of course, they were only to happy to accommodate us."

Karen stood, mouth gaping and arms crossing her chest. She squeaked, "What would my parents and them possibly have in common? And why had they come?" Karen searched her mother's face, and it was blank.

Jud tilted his head and placed a hand on Karen's shoulder. He straightened himself and waved, giving farewells as Karen's parents and newly made friends laughed and stepped into the cab, giving orders to the cabbie, and saying, "Airport."

Karen's mind whirled. Her parents had arranged a flight from Ohio where they had an hour's stopover in Atlanta. And then they went on to Florida. Donald hollered out the cab window, "Bahamas, here we come!"

The ladies were giggling as they hung on to their hats.

Karen let out a long sigh and leaned on the doorjamb. Sara came and looped arms with her best friend. Karen gave her a quick hug and whispered, "Thank you."

"Welcome. What are friends for?" Hand in hand, they entered the living room. The men shared a secret bond.

Karen thought, *Kindred spirits.*

The men smiled and held out their hands for the ladies to join them.

Karen said, "Together, we are a force to be reckoned with." She let a little giggle escape and quickly slipped her arms around Jud.

Jud's parents came and surrounded him. Karen watched as Sylvia and Jon touched Sara's elbow and continued to talk with a now-more-relaxed Ken.

Mariah's suitcase was in hand and her much loyal son in the other. J. J. carried three suitcases and juggled a tote bag as he set them at the front door. He then came alongside Mariah.

Karen made her escape and took her hanky and blew her nose.

Everyone was leaving. It was hard to watch, and her hormones weren't helping. She looked over at Ken smiling with his dad and holding a reluctant Mariah in his arms. Karen glanced over at her husband. He had thrown his head back laughing at something his father said, and his mother and his stepmother were gasping. Both ladies were shaking their hands. Karen saw Eli looking around, and their eyes met.

Eli strolled over to Karen, quietly saying, "You look beautiful for not having much sleep. The wedding you prepared was wonderful. You're so talented and kind." He clicked his fingers. "Now that pair, Claudia and Jack, they are something. She's really bright and funny, and he is so calm."

Karen focused on Eli's features. They spoke volumes of sincerity.

"Please keep in touch with Joan and me. We would really appreciate hearing from you. And please, by all means, let us know about the little one or ones." His brown eyes lifted and were dancing. Eli clasped both his hands over Joan's and brought her into the circle with Jud.

At the door, Joan shook Karen's hand, paused, and touched her cheek. She held her head to the side for Jud to kiss her cheek. So low one could barely hear, she said, "Karen, dear, call me. Let us know about the pregnancy. You are glowing." She touched Karen's cheek once again and was out the door. Eli towered over Joan and held her arm like she was a china doll.

Tom stood talking and joked about bank business. Then he spoke about the devoted Miss Phyler. And then in his gruff voice, he said, "You've become quite a man, Jud."

Dora gazed adoringly at Tom. Karen caught her hand. Dora glanced at her and flashed a big white smile, giving Karen's hand a squeeze.

Tom said, "Jud, Karen, Luke, and Luci, please." He raised his eyebrows and glanced at Karen's stomach, and then he continued. "Come visit us. Take a real vacation. I believe one is needed." Tom affectionately clapped his son on the back and said to him, "I love you, and I'm very proud of you."

Jud's brows pinched together. "We need a vacation, do we?" He chuckled. A few more exchanges were made before Tom and Dora left. Karen blew kisses and stood with Jud's arm around her waist, watching the car until the red and white taillights disappeared from their sight.

Jud grinned. As he bent and lifted Karen up in his arms and swung her around, he said, "Mrs. Day, I love you." He let her down and swatted her on the bottom. "Let's see when our next guests arrive."

Ken flagged Karen and Jud over to join his family and J. J. Talking was easy enough. Sylvia stood with Jon, holding hands. He offered Sylvia his handkerchief.

Sylvia said, "Miechael, you have really changed in the past months. Soon, you will be towering over your mother. I think being a cowboy becomes you. How do you and your uncle Ken get along?"

Miechael tipped his hat. "Oh, he'll do. Sam's not bad either." A sneaky smile was lifting his lips.

Sylvia looked over at Mariah. She noticed J. J.'s arm was around her shoulder. He appeared to be offering shelter. Sylvia took a breath. "Ken, Mariah, please listen to your mother."

Ken moved from one foot to the other, wearing a puzzled look. Mariah distanced herself from J. J. Ken reached for his sister's hand. Mariah looked up at him, bit her lip, and entwined her hand in his. They faced their mother and at the same time said, "What?"

Sylvia, still holding Jon's hand, cleared her throat. "J. J., stay. This concerns you also." Sylvia motioned them to the sofas and sat down. She began. "Ken, I'm proud of your ownership in the disputes you've had with your father." Sylvia put her hand up and said, "Mariah, leaving Miechael with your brother for the school year is wise, but it was a hard decision. And you know it will cultivate him further as a person." Sylvia crossed her feet. "J. J., thank you for giving space to our Mariah so she can further her career and see if that is the path she wants. And for not interfering with your opinions on the raising of her son, Miechael. J. J., we have seen great maturity from you over the year. Your sister, Eurlene, said you're up for a promotion at her bank to cochair in New York. That's quite an accomplishment."

J. J. walked over to Sylvia and stated, "Thank you for your concerns, but I may be buying my own company and not moving foreword in the banking business."

Karen returned, carrying in a pitcher of iced tea and snacks. She offered each one a glass. Jud took the tray, set it down, and took Karen's hand. They each took a seat.

"Mariah, my sweet Mariah, you need to advance with your commitments and decide next year's placement for Miechael's school term. Schooling abroad will also help develop him and give him the extra nutriment he will need in life. Dear Mariah, you need to live in the present and let your past fade. You need to trust in God's leading. And why not take a chance with J. J."

Sylvia moved, and all followed her lead. "Jud, we've known you a long, long time." She touched his cheek.

Karen was surprised to see Jud turning red. He placed a finger at his neck as if choking. Karen patted his back.

"Yes, ma'am, we have."

"Well, Jud, I'm glad you and Ken have remained friends, and it's great that you help one another. I couldn't ask for a better second son." Sylvia blew her nose.

Jud hugged Sylvia and held her. Jud said, "As you know, I didn't have the most affectionate mother, but I know in her bizarre way that she loves me." He let out a sigh. "Sylvia, you've shown me by your life how a mother, a wife, and a woman is to be, and thank you." In the same breath, he added, "My Karen is all of these."

Karen, Sara, Sylvia, and Mariah cried and laughed. The back door slammed, and a boisterous voice said, "Hey, where's everyone at?" Karen jerked around and saw Claudia. "What brings you and Jack in?"

"Well, we hoped we would get to say goodbye to baby girl. And where's her husband, Ken?" Raising her arm, she said, "Karen, will you ship my stuff and garb to my farm?" Claudia glanced up at Jack and squeezed his hand then said, "Our farm."

Karen nodded, and Sara clung to Claudia and told her what a great bride she was and how happy they all were for her and Jack.

Claudia tried to whisper. "He's wonderful." And Claudia squeezed deepened on Jack's arm, blushing.

Jack drew nearer and hung on to Claudia as if she would get blown away at any moment. "We're off to Kentucky. I'm taking my blushing bride home." He turned to Jud and Ken. "Men, I can set up a plan for my studies from anywhere, but you know where to plant your feet when you listen and are called. I've been blessed. he indicated with outward hands—my wife. Isn't she the best?"

Blushing, Claudia thumbed her bibs and slapped Jack on the back. "Come on, the train won't wait."

Jack beamed from ear to ear. "Got to love her." Then he turned to Sara and leaned over. "I'm glad you're doing so well, but God sure has a strange way of bringing people together. Doesn't he?"

Sara hugged Claudia again for a long time. Claudia broke and backed away, saying, "Baby girl, hang on to your man. Claudia trod heavily with her foot. Jack looked into her eyes and kissed her boldly. "Snookums, let's go."

Karen thought, *What a sight. It reminds me of the nursery rhyme, "Jack Sprat could eat no fat. His wife could eat no lean." I should tell Jud. Well, later maybe.*

"Hello, darling. Did I lose you?"

Karen lifted up her chin and slowly smiled. "Try?" She saw the late afternoon was finally calming down. Karen said, "Jud, how about you and Ken playing a few numbers before he and his folks leave?"

J. J. stepped forward. "I play a mean harmonica. How about it?" He twirled it in his fingers.

Karen looked over at Mariah. She hunched her shoulders and rolled her huge hazel eyes. Then she motioned to Miechael to listen and watch. Miechael stood in front of his mother with her arms wrapped around him; they swayed as the men sang and played.

Timmy, Matthew, Luke, and Luci clapped hands, keeping in time to the rhythm.

Miechael said to J. J. when he stepped away from the other men, "You're pretty good for a city boy."

J. J. saw that smiles were turning into laughter. "Not you too, Miechael." He tousled the lad's black hair.

Sylvia hugged Mariah and pulled Ken to her. "Call and come see your mother and father. And bring J. J." She also broke into laughter.

Jon patted J. J. on the back. "Now see what I go through."

Karen and Jud held hands as their friends bade them farewell and promised to write and call. Miechael left with Ken and Sara as well as Timmy. Timmy grabbed on to Matthew and whispered, "Be nice. Mom is going to talk to Dad about a little girl." Timmy turned once again. He winked and spoke over the group. "Luci, write to me. I would like that."

For a brief moment, every eye was on Luci. She smiled then giggled.

Luke frowned. "Hey, what's that all about? He's my friend too! Luci?"

Karen squeezed Jud's hand, and each one placed a hand on the twins. "Anyone for a swim?"

Jud touched Karen's mouth. "Meet me at the pool?"

"I have a lot of cleaning up to do." She tapped her foot. "And then there's dinner."

"Ahem!"

"Sam! Louise! What happened?"

"Jud, the missus and I went ahead and cleaned the entertainment center under the apartments. I lifted the straw and loaded it onto the truck, and we will haul it to Ken's place."

"Karen, the decorations such as the horseshoes and all with the cactus glasses are sitting on the kitchen counter."

Louise handed the basket over to Karen.

"Would you like some cold cuts to eat before the trip?"

"Karen, we would like some of that mint chocolate iced tea to enjoy along the way." Sam winked at Louise. "We are in no hurry getting to Sara and Ken's. We're taking in a few sights along the way."

Louise just waved him on and blushed.

Luke placed a hand on Sam. "Would you and Louise like to swim?"

Sam covered his mouth so as not to show his chuckle. "Well, I think I could take a dip."

"Let's get our suits on."

Karen motioned as she went into the kitchen to check on things. Sam nodded. Louise snapped an apron. "Like old times. Yes?"

"Thanks, Louise. I don't know when I've been happier."

"Karen, how are your mother and father really doing? I didn't even get a chance to thank her for all her hard work she did in helping me with the auction. I miss our talking, but things do change."

Karen gave Louise a quick sweep. She saw Louise's facial features go from a pinched brow to uplifted eyes. "Louise, I'll tell Mother. Have you and Sam decided where you'll be living now? Wait just a minute." Karen went to the pantry. "Here, Louise, this is our present for you and Sam."

Tears formed in Louise's eyes. "Karen, that wasn't necessary."

"Just say thank you." Karen embraced the older woman, and new feelings emerged.

"Oh, Karen, thank you both."

Louise dried the last pan, and Karen turned to the whistling tea kittle. Sam appeared from swimming. "I'll be right down after a quick shower."

The ladies were still talking when Sam stepped into the kitchen, looking refreshed.

He untied Louise's apron and kissed her cheek. "Thanks, Karen, for the goodies you packed in our picnic basket. We'll enjoy them. Oh, you've already included the fresh brewed tea. Well, thanks again." They hugged.

Jud and the twins were changed and scurried to give goodbyes to Mr. and Mrs. Month. Louise hugged Luci and then Luke. "Take good care of your sister, Luke."

"Ah, Mrs. Month? I really don't need care, but thank you." And Luci curtsied.

Karen held out a finger to correct Luci, but she was stopped by that look Louise gave her.

Louise stepped over and hugged Karen. "She's growing up."

Karen nodded.

Louise continued. "Did you see the way she looked at Timmy?" She squeezed Karen's arm and then reached for Jud.

Sam held the door open for his wife, and Louise slid in and looked out his truck window and waved.

Once again, Karen and Jud gazed at taillights far down the road.

"Mom, after you read to us, may Luci and I watch a movie?"

"I'll pop some popcorn, but I'll get the book. Let's read."

After the open-ended answer time, Luke said, "Dad, I have a question about banking." He blew out a breath. "I want to be just like you." Luke smiled.

Karen shifted her attention to Jud.

Jud said, "We need to sit down, son, and go over your subjects scheduled this year in school and highlight the most important ones. But that doesn't get you out of sports."

Luci got on her knees and whispered in her mother's ear, "Do you think I should be keeping a diary?"

"Well, why not, sweetheart?" Karen glanced at her and thought, *Luci is blushing.*

"Mom, bend over. I don't want Dad or Luke to hear."

"What, Luci?"

"Mom, can we talk later when we're alone? It's about…" She spelled Timmy's name out as if there was silence in her whispering.

Karen fanned herself with a magazine. "Sure." She nodded. "Anytime."

Jud fiddled with the logs in the fireplace as Luke added on another log. "Karen, why don't we get ready for bed and meet back in here for the movie?"

"Last one downstairs is a rotten egg," Timmy yelled out.

Luci added, "Dad, start the tape."

"I want to watch this one."

"No, this one. Hey, give it back."

Karen mused and was glad to know they weren't so grown up after all.

Jud patted the seat.

Karen entered the room. "What are we watching?" She waited, but there was no answer.

"Mom, can you bring the popcorn over here too?" There was a long pause. He added. "For Luci and me?" Luke saw his mother standing there, tapping her foot, and he rose. He seized the bowl, took a few bites, and tossed Luci a few grains. Reaching his hands out, he offered, "Popcorn, anyone?"

Jud threw a pillow and then a second one. "What do you think? Luke?"

The movie was paused while Luke and his dad wrestled. Luci shook her head and stared into her mother's slanting blue eyes. She sat for only a moment and nestled. "Mother, they're so juvenile."

Karen watched and then touched Jud's shoulder. "Did I hear someone say uncle? Time's ticking." Karen patted the seat and batted her eyes.

Jud obeyed. "Put another log on the fire, Luke. Get the lights." He placed an arm around Karen and crossed his feet at his ankles. "Action." Another pillow was tossed, and giggles filled the air.

13

Several months passed, and winter's wrath was in full swing. And yet a heavenly white purity was felt throughout the states. Fellow citizens traveling for work or pleasure were hit by delays. Schools were canceled, leaving mothers to plan crafts for their children or read to them. Outside play was limited.

The snow had fallen to an unheard-of twenty inches in Columbus, Ohio. The city was stranded for two complete days. A lot of electrical power was out. The newspaper writers were having a field day in reporting.

New York's regular, feet-deep snow came down, but it didn't seem to slow anyone down.

Mississippi's snow report only gave signs of scattered flurries, but anything could stop the state's movements.

An unexpected blizzard came through Idaho and mostly paralyzed the state. Some homebodies could tune in their TV or radios to know what was going on in the world.

Sara, of all people, had phone service. She called Karen on the landline, which crackled and hissed throughout their conversation. Sara said, "Brown and Brown's attorney, who stayed at the bed-and-breakfast, made a trip to Mississippi to see her." The lines popped, but Sara carried on. "They're interested in purchasing my purse business. Karen, what should I do?"

"Would there be party plans?" Karen sighed.

"No, Karen, I'm afraid not. Brown and Brown would be the distributor. I would be selling my business completely."

"Have you talked with Ken, Jud, or Spencer? How silly, of course Ken would know."

The line crackled and went *buzz, buzz, buzz*. Karen unwillingly hung up the phone. She still had questions, but she needed to get ready for another purse show. She complained, "Two shows. Why did I cram them back to back"?

Footsteps came down the hall, and a voice called out.

Karen said, "Mother?"

"My dear, your feet are already beginning to swell. Would you like me to go along with you this afternoon and help out?"

After a deep sigh, Karen answered, "Will you drive, please? I'm tired before we've even started." Karen hunched her shoulders. "I really don't know why," she added as she stroked her stomach. Both ladies laughed.

Kate wiggled her index finger and shook her head. "I think this purse business is too much for you, especially after the new one arrives."

"Mother, you may not need to be concerned about the party plan much longer."

Karen turned and saw Jud standing there. "Jud, everyone has checked out from the bed-and-breakfast, except for one guest. You'll need to heat the casserole and serve him. As for Luke, Luci, and yourself, fix the hot dogs and serve the potato salad on the second shelf in the ice box."

"Okay." His lips turned upward. "I think I can handle tonight. You be careful. Oh, Kate, you're going with Karen. Great. Well, ladies, have fun. See you later, Karen." He nodded and backed away.

Karen was delighted that her mother attended the parties. At the first show, Karen preceded without too much pain. But by the second purse show, Karen's feet were swollen and had begun to cramp.

Kate helped the ladies with their orders and asked Karen to slide the small box of left purses into the car and stay. Karen gave a sickly smile and sit down. She bit her lip as her shoes were pushed off. She noticed her feet had overrun the pumps. In the car on the way home, she couldn't get comfortable. She held her hands up. "Look, Mother, my hands are pudgy, and they ache."

"Karen, are you carrying only one baby?"

Karen's eyes narrowed as she glanced her mother's way. "Dr. March let me see the outline, and he assured me there is one, but there would be another scan next month for review. Maybe it's just a big baby."

"The swelling must be from the lack of elevation. You need bed rest." Kate gave a thin smile and drove in silence.

"Mother, what I wanted to say earlier is, Sara received an offer for her purse business. She called me this morning. Her lines were filled with birds again." Karen chuckled.

"Oh, did they go down again?"

"Yes, Mother."

Kate resumed talking. "Well, the sale of the purse business may be a blessing in disguise. Especially the way the bed-and-breakfast reserved bookings are occurring." Kate touched Karen's arm and added. "And now with your and Sara's baby's too-soon arrival."

Karen rested her head, and her eyelids seemed heavy. "What did you say?" Her voice trailed off into a whisper.

An hour later, Kate pulled in the drive, parked, and touched Karen's shoulder. "We're home."

Although sitting felt rewarding, she hadn't catnapped long enough. Karen opened the door, and the freezing air made her sharply awake.

Karen heard his voice. "Wait."

She closed the door, not wanting to push her pumps back on, and waited. "Oh, Jud, I forgot how miserable I was being pregnant until now. I'm like a pin cushion."

He lifted her with ease, and she melted with his touch as he carried her to their room. "Dear, don't worry about a thing. Our guests are cared for as are the kids. We went swimming while you were out, and they begged for bed. Here, slip into this and rest." He lifted her legs and said, "Place your feet on top of the pillows. Perhaps sleep will come." Jud kissed her forehead and pulled the spread over her. Karen wiggled then snuggled deeper under the covers as he went out of the bedroom.

He moved down the stairs, taking several steps, and answered the phone. "How did you get through?"

"Through the phone company's patchwork. I'm not sure for how long, though."

"Ken, is anything wrong?"

"No, I have wonderful news."

"Go on."

"The Brown and Brown's attorney is buying Sara's purse business. She's excited. And guess what? Sam sold his five-plus-acre farm to Spencer. Eurlene will be surprised."

"Wow." Jud paced back and forth. "Maybe I don't know Eurlene like I thought. I'm speechless."

"Jud, you need to be here for the closing of Sara's purse enterprise." The line crackled. "Oh, I almost forgot. We're having a baby girl, and Sara has been so sick. It's nothing like when she carried the boys. I'm so glad Louise is here to help us. And then Sara has mood swings."

"Ken?" There wasn't any dial tone. Jud pushed his hands in his pockets, jiggling some coins. He deliberated while pacing. He worked up a sweat and spoke, "How am I going to tell Karen that Eurlene is moving to old Sam's place, which is in the same state and is fairly close to Ken and Sara's residence? Although Eurlene is married to Spencer." He paced some more. "It still won't matter. Eurlene will never be far away enough for Karen's peace of mind. Karen's green-eyed monster roared while we were in Paris. And she is not well enough to hear this news at all. And Karen's so pregnant."

"Jud?" He jerked.

"Good evening, Kate." Jud rolled his shoulders.

"You mention Eurlene's name. What's this about her and Mississippi?" She wagged a finger. "My advice to you, Jud is communication. Be truthful always. The sooner your wife knows, the better!"

Jud sighed. "I will." He rolled his eyes.

Kate suddenly tapped her forehead. "Mississippi would be the perfect place for Mariah's wedding." Kate motioned to the phone. "You finished?"

Jud waved her on with his hand. "Be my guest." His brow slanted as he went on his way. "Wedding?" He hit his head. "Whoa Jud, communication is not going to be a problem again." He rubbed his chin. "I need to speak with Karen first thing in the morning about my attending Sara's closing and, um, Eurlene's new place." He twisted his hands as he walked into the office. He opened his briefcase.

Kate dialed and instantly said, "Hello, Lady Ma Mere. This is Kate Page. I know it's only eight o'clock in the morning, but I had to call." She waited as asked, pulled out a stool, and tittered like a schoolgirl.

"No, your timing is perfect, my dear. The duke is still lying down. What's on your mind?"

"I overheard a phone conversation between Ken and Jud. Spencer has bought Sam's place in Mississippi. A surprise gift for Eurlene. Now my purpose in calling is that I thought if you and Sylvia agreed, we could possibly arrange and pull off Mariah's wedding there."

"Would it be too remote, Kate?"

"Well, it would be out of the public's eye, but the town is bound to have a suitable church. And Louise is quite a cook, and not to brag, so am I. We could also plan the reception. What do you think?"

"My, let's do some secretive research," Lady Ma Mere whispered as though someone might overhear her words. "We need to be sure Sam sold the place to Spencer, and we need to see Spencer's new place. Wonder how soon he will be presenting the news to Eurlene? There are measurements needed. And will there be enough room for everyone we invite to the wedding reception? How are we going to decorate?" There was a slight pause before Lady Ma Mere said, "Let's find out if there is a church close by within ten to twenty miles from Old Sam's place. Oh, and I'm so on board with Mariah getting married. Kate, this wedding needs to happen next month."

"Why so soon?" Kate said.

Lady Ma Mere reverted to her usual tone. "The duke and I are scheduled to host more gala events, give speeches, and make personal appearances, so travel will be our life after next month for the next year." She coughed. "You know J. J. lost popularity with Mariah because of the ladies flocking after him and with all his public appearances, per Eurlene's call." She sighed. "And Kate, Mariah is determined with her modeling. She revels in the spotlight and attention showered on her. The fast lane is not kind to one after awhile. Mariah needs to settle down and have a good father figure for Miechael, and she needs more babies and lots of them. She's not getting any younger." You could hear her fingers tapping. "I'll call Sylvia. Can you book a flight out for tomorrow? We don't have any time to lose."

"Oh, Lady Ma Mere, what about Mariah's wishes? Shouldn't we consult her?"

"Don't give Mariah another thought, Kate. Like I said, I'm calling Sylvia. You just be on that flight to Mississippi and don't forget to book our rooms. Ciao!"

Kate was in a hot mess of a dilemma. What was she to say to Donald or, for that matter, Jud or Karen? Kate decided it was best to leave a note. She placed it by the phone.

Dear Donald,

I'll call you later. Sorry you were out and I missed you, but Lady Ma Mere needs my help with a new project. See to Karen's needs. She should have lots of bed rest and pampering. Jud, you should watch after the kids and take care of the architectural structuring going on in the bed-and-breakfast's new third floor.

Love you,
Kate

The plane landed at the airport, and the taxi was on standby. She said, "I'm so grateful for smooth connections." She waved her hankie, and the cabbie took her luggage. "Where to, miss?"

"The Baptist church in Leakesville, and then to a bed-and-breakfast located in town."

The cabbie nodded, shut Kate's door, slid behind the wheel, and pulled the lever down. The cab meter ticked away. It was only a short drive from the airport to the church. Kate opened the door, and as she got off from the cab, she motioned to the cabbie to wait. She marveled at the sight before her. The church was painted a marvelous, striking white. And it shone over the neatly repaired and well-laid lumber. Its age had held with the times, and the overall appearance was exquisite. A cemetery stood across the road. As she walked, she noticed the nicely graveled circular driveway. Kate clutched her purse. "My, it's like stepping back in time." She placed her hands to her chest. "How quaint and perfect!"

The cabbie said, "I'm keeping the meter running."

Kate nodded. She had deliberately worn a loose-fitted dress of the era with its matching jacket. She liked hats and wore them toward the front of her head, neatly placed with pins and a comb. Kate chose pumps for this adventure.

She walked up the flight of steps. The church appeared beckoning and warm. The wraparound porch seemed endless. Kate scanned the sides and saw the beautifully dug beds where wild flowers and bright, delightful roses would bloom, if it were spring. Kate crossed her arms around her closer as the nippy air blew around her.

She peeked through the long, narrow stained glass windows beside the mission style front door. Kate paused before she knocked, but the doors surprisingly opened. She quickly stepped inside and looked up to the ceiling, which appeared to be floating toward the clouds.

Stretching across the ceiling were wood crossbeams. It was charming. She took a few more steps and noticed the old seats were made of hand-carved cherry wood. However the pews were white washed. The building was definitely impressive. The clip-clopping of heels gave Sylvia and Lady Ma Mere away. Kate saw both women touch the pews. They twisted and turned. "Ah, beautiful." Lady Ma Mere clasped her hands. "This is the perfect place for a wedding. Ladies, what will be our plan of action and the decorations?" She clenched her teeth. "We'll need to speak with the person in charge here and ask about renting the building."

Sylvia said, "I called Spencer, and he confirmed that he bought Old Sam's place. I can call him back and ask if we can have Mariah and J. J.'s reception there." While waiting, she added, "You know Eurlene will have the place up to snuff and then some." Sylvia touched her mother's hand. "Lady Ma Mere, Eurlene needs to work with us and work on J. J."

Kate turned, staring at the two women. "Lady Ma Mere, you told Sylvia about Spencer's purchase?"

She waved her hand. "What's the big deal? We're here now, and aren't we in this together?"

Kate turned up her nose. "I wanted to break the news."

Lady Ma Mere let out a sigh. "Too late."

"Come on, you two, we need to plan how to get J. J. and Mariah here. They will need their marriage license when they arrive, for there is a three-day waiting period after they apply."

It got quiet. Kate said, "I wonder if Eurlene even knows about Sam's place?"

Kate looked at the ladies. "That's our starting point."

A sudden scuffle broke their conversation. An older, balding but white-headed gentleman walked toward them. His arms were behind his back, his coat was unbuttoned, and he was wearing an angelic smile. "May I help you ladies?"

Lady Ma Mere stiffened. She offered him her hand. "We want to rent the church. It's for my granddaughter's wedding. Are there openings for this coming month?"

He chuckled. "Oh, there are many dates available, for we are but a dying congregation. We are of thirty-five strong. When would you like this gala event to happen?"

"Are you the minister?" Lady Ma Mere cracked a smile. "This next month, but we are not quite sure of the date. Perhaps we could book the entire month. How much do you charge for the building and your services?"

"This request, I must say, is quite unusual." He rocked back and forth on his feet. "I am the minister. My rule is I would like to meet with the couple-to-be one week prior to their wedding for counseling. And a donation would be most helpful. We would like to get our pew seats recovered as well as the pads to the piano bench and organ. They are in rough condition, but our funds are limited."

Kate moved a few feet away and spoke privately with Sylvia and Lady Ma Mere. "Sylvia, why don't you and your mother, along with the minister, select the fabric for the seating, and I'll call Louise. I'll see if she's free. Perhaps we can reupholster the seats and cover the benches."

14

Kate said, "Lady Ma Mere, you need to talk with Spencer and Eurlene for their part in the reception."

Lady Ma Mere nodded and said, "Kate, Sylvia, I know what I need to do, but can you two carry things through here?"

"Mother, don't look down your nose at us." Sylvia's thin lips softened. She touched her mother's arm. "We're in this together, remember?"

"Sylvia, here's my decision. You need to arrange a visit at Mariah's. And encourage your daughter to select a wedding dress." She waved her royal hand. "I don't care what reason you come up with, but this cannot be put off. You also need a reason for her to come back with you to Mississippi."

Sylvia sighed. "The tangled web we weave."

Lady Ma Mere reached for her purse. "Here, sir, is a check for $1,000. It should cover the church rental and clerical fees for the month." She looked back at the pews. "What colors and fabric texture were you thinking of for the seats? Or do you make the final decisions?" Lady Ma Mere faced Kate. "She'll take care of the seats and the bench covers. May we have a key?"

The minister beamed and took Lady Ma Mere's hand. He was still patting it when he said, "Ma'am the church is always open." He blushed somewhat. "I'm usually here. I have an office and sleeping area in the back. Please drop in, and thank you again for the offer. Oh, the color for fabric should be blue like the sky. Everything else in fabric notions will be left up to you and your excellent taste." His smile broadened. "Again, thank you, ladies and Lady Ma Mere."

Lady Ma Mere slid her hand from his and had a smile on her face, which didn't quite reach her eyes. She turned and herded the other two ladies out. "Let's get in the cab."

Lady Ma Mere placed a hand over Kate's while addressing the cabbie. "Where is a suitable place to eat around here?"

Sylvia muttered, "Mother, why are you always taking charge. You're so controlling."

Kate reached over and touched her arm and gave Sylvia a squeeze.

The cabbie motioned as he pulled away. "The one and only fine dining is next to the bed-and-breakfast."

There was complete silence. He parked in front of the bed-and-breakfast and removed their luggage. Kate thanked the cabbie, paid the fare, and left a large tip. She suggested to Sylvia and Lady Ma Mere to go ahead and find them a seat as she would soon join them. .

"Whew." Kate rang a bell and a middle-aged woman appeared. She smiled. "How may I help you?"

Kate took a deep breath. "I would like to book three suites for twenty-four hours and possibly longer. Is that a problem?" She glazed into the sober eyes of the owner.

The woman winced, but her smile remained intact. "It's sixty-five dollars per night per person, and if you upgrade for a longer stay, we can oblige."

Kate reached into her purse. "Here's my credit card for our reservations. The other two ladies are Sylvia News and Lady Ma Mere. And please, we don't wish for any publicity." Kate's eyebrows rose.

The woman on the other side of the counter screamed. "We're rooming a celebrity."

Kate laughed and waited.

"Sorry. What else is needed, ma'am?"

"Is there someone available to help me with the entire luggage?"

"Yes, ma'am, we'll take care of everyone's luggage, and here are the keys. Ma'am, sign in here please. Is there anything you or the ladies would like to have in your rooms when you arrive?"

"A pot of hot tea would be nice, miss. Thank you." Kate turned, walked up stairway, and sought out the rooms. She switched on the lights and was pleased. She walked through the adjoining doors and said, "Everything is excellent."

Kate entered her room and rang downstairs for aid in connecting a call to her friend, Louise.

"Hello, Louise. This is Kate. I'm so glad you answered. I need your help. Keep my call secret. Tell me. How is Sara doing? And can you get away? Remember, this is hush-hush."

"Sara is all right for now. How long would I be needed Kate, and for what?"

"The place isn't far. And it's still in Mississippi, and it's for major sewing for about two to three weeks. Can't really talk on the phone. You know how walls have ears. Can you come?

Louise chuckled. "This sounds delicious."

"Next week, Tuesday. I'll tell you more when you get here at the bed-and-breakfast." Kate heard Louise clapping her hands. "Now mum's the word."

"Okay."

"Bye."

The three ladies—Kate, Sylvia, and Lady Ma Mere—hatched a plan.

Lady Ma Mere was in a cab headed to Old Sam's place to talk with Spencer about Mariah and J. J.'s reception.

Sylvia caught a flight out to New York. She had never surprised her daughter with a visit, but she hoped to convince

Mariah to postpone any modeling events and to rally Mariah into a wedding—her own.

Kate stayed in Mississippi and waited on Louise. During her stay, she also persuaded her husband, Donald, into coming. She said, "I need you to come up with a plan, for Jon needs to be supportive of the marriage and stand by J. J. and Mariah."

Everyone had an agenda for all the work to be accomplished. The ladies agreed to touch base with Kate by phone, calling her at the bed-and-breakfast in Mississippi. She would be instructed on the updates and any gossip.

"Hello, Eurlene?"

"Spencer, where have you been? I've called everywhere for you. Today I had just missed you for you had already left."

A smile lifted at the corners of his mouth and reached his eyes. "Checking up on me were you?" He could hear her thinking.

"No, well, I miss you."

"My Eurlene, I bought you a present. I miss you likewise."

"What? Where are you?"

Spencer burst out laughing. "You're so suspicious. Please, my pet, there is no one I could or would ever love but you. And this is so out of character for you." He heard her heel hit the tiled floor.

"Spencer!"

"Red, I'm teasing."

"It's Eurlene. Now what?"

"As I was saying, I need for you to get coverage at the bank. Call Tom, Jud's father. I want you here in Mississippi by tomorrow."

"Why on earth would I want to come to a forsaken place like that? And certainly not for a stay? You must be out of your ever-loving mind."

"Eurlene?" There was no doubt in his mind she had hung up on him. Shaking his head, he said, "I know she will come. Curiosity killed the cat, and she is every bit filled with curiosity."

There was a continuous honking noise. Spencer stepped from the house and gaped. He was not a man to show surprise or be taken off guard. But there he stood gazing at a cab and seeing the Grand Lady Ma Mere. She appeared as if she had been on a cover of a magazine. Spencer waltzed to her side. "Well, Lady Ma Mere, to what do I owe the pleasure of your company?" he asked as he took her hand and kissed it.

She stood for a moment, and cleared her throat before speaking. She eyed him from head to toe and said, "You appearance is certainly different, Spencer."

Spencer's lips lifted. "Lady Ma Mere, again, why are you here?"

"May we step in out of the cold? I can see my breath." For drama, she clutched her fur coat.

Spencer bowed and held a hand up for the cabbie to wait. "This way, ma'am."

Lady Ma Mere stripped off her coat and began walking through his house. She stretched her hands over the fireplace and remarked, "This is a very rustic place. I like its structure and character. Is your purchase for the farm completed with Sam?"

Spencer blinked and squinted. "First, how did you know? And second, what business is it of yours, Lady Ma Mere?"

Lady Ma Mere took his arm. "Do you have any tea? I would like a cup of steamy black tea."

"Nothing fancy, but yes, I can make you a cup of tea." He added water to the teakettle and stared at this woman sitting at the long table and smiling.

Spencer served his guest and reached for bottled water before he straddled a chair. Another minute or two passed. "Well?" Spencer said.

"When will Eurlene be present?"

"And the reason you're asking?"

Lady Ma Mere waved her arm in the air. "With Mariah and J. J. getting married next month"—she paused and looked Spencer in the eye and then took a sip of tea—"I wanted their reception to be here at Old Sam's place."

Spencer tapped his forehead. "Who's getting married?" He let out a deep breath. "You did say Mariah and J. J. Is that correct?"

"Yes, indeed I did. I need to discuss with Eurlene about the furnishings and her décor. When will she be here?"

Spencer stood up and began pacing. "Lady Ma Mere, this now is my place, but Eurlene is not aware of the purchase. It's a surprise for her. And it's a place in which she can get away from the city to relax. I didn't know about her brother's wedding." He tilted his black Stetson back on his head.

Not waiting for him to comment further, Lady Ma Mere said, "It is all right to have the reception here then by next month? I'll keep in touch in a couple of weeks about the decorations." She stood up, smiled, and handed her coat to him. At the cab, she thanked him for all his help and left him with his hands on his hips. Lady Ma Mere spoke loudly from the rolled-down window of the cab. "Oh, Spencer, the wedding is also a surprise." She waved her hankie.

Spencer had to sit down on the porch steps. He asked himself, "What had just happened here? I have never lost control ever in my life—well, since becoming an attorney and maybe, Eurlene." He wasn't much of a praying man, but he clasped his hands, lowered his head, and prayed. *Lord, help us.*

Spencer heard the phone ring. "Hello?"

There was no hi back. Eurlene just said, "I'll be there tonight. What road do I take after the turnoff after Ken's?"

"You're driving?"

"Give me directions and quit asking silly questions."

"Eurlene, I can come into—"

"What crossroads?"

Spencer said, "There isn't any crossroads. You need to look out for an old building with a faded red sign saying 'Feed-store.' Turn to your immediate right. Go five miles. You'll see a caution sign posted. Make a sharp turn left. Come two more miles down the narrow road. There are only three houses, and the house on your left is ours. Eurlene, I didn't know Mariah and J. J. were getting married?"

"Spencer, have you lost your mind? I'll see you later! Bye."

He stared at the silent phone. Pacing, he thought, *I'll call Ken. He will know what's going on.* Spencer placed the call, but Sam answered the phone. "Sam, hi. I've called for Ken. Is he there?"

"No, Spencer, he isn't. He's not at the bank either. Can I help?"

"Don't know if you can or not, Sam. Do you know anything about a wedding?"

"Spencer, Louise mentioned a vague reference to a wedding, but she said, 'Mum is the word.'"

"Is Louise available?"

"No." Sam sighed. "She's with Kate at the church fixing seats or something."

"Do you think Ken knows anything?"

"I don't know. Why, Spencer?"

"I had a strange visit from Lady Ma Mere. She hoodwinked me into letting the reception take place here at the farm. As she was leaving, she mentioned the wedding is a surprise. What's that all about?"

Sam began laughing.

Spencer, in his thoughts, knew he needed to get the house in tiptop shape for Eurlene, so he just hung up.

He had the oven on, and the homemade bread was rising. A covered dish was set on top of the stove. He was standing at the sink peeling potatoes when the back door snapped. He took a deep breath before turning, and Eurlene's fragrance wafted through the air.

Over his shoulder, he saw her standing there, not moving and holding a small case in hand. "Darling, you've made great time." He leaned forward and kissed her lips. He saw her shiver. "Eurlene, is everything all right? Come sit and have tea."

She followed him without saying a word. A few sips later, she said, "Spencer, is this my surprise?"

He took her hands and brought her to him. "It is. Let me show you around."

For a moment, she lingered and kissed him back. "I'm perfectly capable of looking after myself. Where's the chef?"

"You were kissing him." He smiled as he went to the stove. "Dinner will be ready in twenty minutes. Want to help set the table?" He knew he was pushing her limits.

Click-clack was all he heard as she muttered, "Get real." Eurlene walked around and made little remarks here and there. She finished looking and entered the kitchen. She stopped and brought her hands to her mouth. There was Spencer who appeared every bit the cowboy, from his hat to his broad shoulders, in a white western shirt, which narrowed at his hips, and form-fitting black jeans. He was wearing leather cowboy boots.

He turned and placed his feet inches apart and crossed his arms. "See anything you like, Red?"

Spencer stood tall at six feet two inches and emitted a confidence she knew so well, seeing him in and out of the courtrooms and in his three-piece business suits. Oh, she liked it all right, but giving in was not in her nature. "Where did you get your getup, cowboy?" Eurlene couldn't help herself as she winked.

Spencer rocked on the heel of his boots and stuck his thumbs in the front pockets of his jeans. He smiled and removed his hat. "Get over here. I thought you missed me."

"I'm hungry now."

He mused. "Me too." His brows arched slightly.

Eurlene looked into the dark wooden cabinet and took out two white china plates. He motioned to the drawer, and she pulled out two complete utensil settings. "Need anything else?"

"Maybe." The aroma filled the air as he came closer carrying the hot, buttery potato casserole dish and homemade bread.

15

Eurlene stood beside a chair, tapping her foot and waiting to be seated. With a snap, Spencer's apron came off. He sat Eurlene down and gave her a teasing kiss.

Eurlene's nose scrunched before she said, "This farm is so remote, and it sits nowhere near nothing." She glared at him. "Spencer, what were you thinking?" Her blue eyes widened and then sparkled. And then she continued. "But first of all, thanks for the gift. And I do love the farm."

Spencer didn't try to make conversation. He only quietly passed the food and nodded when it was necessary. After dinner, he quickly cleared the table and began the chore of dishes. Eurlene slipped in behind him and wrapped her arms around his waist. "No one could be more dashing than you in a suit, Spencer. Well, come to bed with me." Over her shoulder, she said, "I may even help you clean up later."

Spencer immediately turned off the water, wheeled on the heel of his boot, bent, and lifted Eurlene. She wiggled, and a shoe came off. "Spencer, what a nice deed, placing logs in the fireplace." Just then it crackled. After a lingering kiss, she said, "Spencer did you lock our door?"

He rose from the bed on an elbow and looked into her soft blue eyes. "Who are we keeping out?" He ran a thumb down her cheek before removing her other shoe. He carefully kissed each foot and toe.

Eurlene reached for his hand.

Spencer lowered his head and nuzzled her neck. But the lawyer in him couldn't resist. He lowly stated, "What do you know about your brother and Mariah getting married?"

Eurlene wrapped her hands around Spencer's neck and toyed with his nape hair. "Whose wedding?" She placed a kiss on his cheek.

He inhaled and shivered. "J. J.'s."

Eurlene bolted upright. "Spencer, this better be good." She ruffled her red hair and swung her feet to the side. "You sit over there!" She motioned him with her index finger to a wingback chair. "Now, mister, start talking and from the beginning."

"Eurlene, I can talk from the bed."

Her look held him in place, and he obeyed. "Here's what I do know. Lady Ma Mere came here looking for you and wanted to have Mariah and J. J.'s reception here next month in three weeks. As she was leaving, she also said something about the wedding being a surprise."

Eurlene gasped. "You let the Lady Ma Mere in here before this place was decorated?"

A smile broke on his face. "Well, honey, not in here."

Eurlene scooted to the edge of the bed and threw a pillow at him. He pretended to be wounded, calling out, "Ouch!" as he shielded his face.

She scampered to the phone. He followed. "Who are you calling at this late hour? People do sleep!"

"Maybe you."

"Hello? Yes? This is an emergency." She was tapping her nails on the table. "Thanks for taking the call, Ted. Here's the address, and I need you here in the morning." She scanned the room as she continued. "Everything goes except the kitchen table and the oversized four-poster bed. Ted, an advanced design is needed and should be finished in..." She looked at Spencer as he held up three fingers, indicating three weeks. Eurlene cleared her throat and said, "Within two weeks. No delays."

Spencer nodded and stood behind her, resting his hands on her back.

"Now, Eurlene." Ted whined.

"Ted, we have no time. This is a truly an emergency. My little brother is getting married, and the reception is being held here. Guests are attending, such as the Grand Lady and Duke Ma Meres, so do not dillydally! Be here in the morning by seven." Eurlene hung up the phone and patted the bed for Spencer to return.

"Spencer, I wonder if Ken knows anything?"

As Spencer sat down, he said, "I called his house earlier, and Sam thought not. But he informed me that Louise was working with Kate at the church here in town sewing something."

Spencer kissed her cheek.

"Get ready and take me there."

"Now?"

He reached for her arms. "Do you know people here go to bed with the chickens? Come on, Eurlene, we will go to the church in the morning after Ted arrives. Ah, Eurlene, let's snuggle."

Eurlene squirmed under his touch, but she soon surrendered. "Tomorrow is another day." She grabbed his belt loop. "Where did this poster bed come from, cowboy?"

He chuckled. "Well, it's been in storage for years. It belonged to my grandmother. She had two exactly alike. One was left to me, and the other one was left to my dad's brother. The beds, as I was told, were hand-tooled by a Hungarian man. My grandmother had met him in her travels, and I suppose they were considered engaged. But after the beds were delivered to the States and the war broke out, no word ever came from him. My grandmother couldn't find him, so years later, she married someone else, namely, my grandfather." He slid his hand over the engraved headboard.

As an afterthought, he whispered, "My grandfather never let her keep the beds in the house, but he did keep them stored for her. I understand that from time to time, he would find her at the warehouse gazing at them."

Eurlene sat easily on the bed. "Oh, that's so sad." A tear fell. "Your poor grandmother."

Spencer slid in bed. "True, the story is sad, but Grandmother was anything but poor, and my Granddaddy was rich and became even wealthier. Lady Ma Mere has nothing on the old girl."

"I'm glad you were a recipient of one king-size poster bed. Look at me." She made the motions of making a snow angel. "The mattresses feel as though they are filled with feathers. So soft and comfortable."

"Princess, you're floating on a bed of feathers." He whispered. "Eurlene?" Her chest was already steadily heaving up and down. He shook his head and pulled the quilt up and whispered, "At last she sleeps."

The sun emerged through the white fluffy clouds and came into view; it promised to be a picture-perfect day. Spencer watched as Mr. Ted Billings measured, nodded, and followed Eurlene around like a puppy. He checked off his to-do list. It was far too chaotic for Spencer, who was used to total quiet—unless he was in the courtroom. Spencer sipped the last of his coffee and kissed Eurlene. His phone rang. "Hello?"

"Spencer, I glad I reached you. Mr. Brown and Brown's attorney is here in the bank's conference room. I need you to read over their papers."

"Be right there."

Spencer said, "Eurlene, I'm needed at the bank this morning. We'll go into town later." He grazed her lips.

Spencer was in attorney mode. He read their proposal and adjusted a few things. Then said, "If there are no questions, then Sara's purse business is legally yours. Please sign where necessary. Sara will need to sign the necessary papers. Then they will mail them out to you."

Wait!"

Spencer's eyes narrowed.

Ken handed him the paperwork again, and Spencer skimmed through them. He looked up a couple of times and bit his lower lip for Sara had already signed them. He signed his name and stamped the legal seal. He rose and made a copy to place in Sara's files. Spencer handed the work back to Ken. "Give the company their copy."

Brown and Brown's attorney said, "Papers will be posted today, and again, thanks for your promptness." The attorney clasped his briefcase and quietly left.

Spencer glanced to the right and saw Donald. "Hi, what are you doing here?"

"I came to spend some quality time with my wife." He tapped Ken on the shoulder. "And I wanted to go over the house plans with Ken. He and Jon are building one for Louise and Sam."

Spencer turned and directed his speech to Ken. "Jon's coming, Ken?"

"Yes, it's down season in Idaho. And when I mentioned that Sam needed a house built, I think his ears went up."

Donald shook Ken's arm. "Better call Jud. He needs to be here for the check to close out Sara's business account. Now the business is sold, and Spencer holds the check. And speaking of Sara, how is she doing?"

Ken sat down. "My head is spinning."

Spencer raised his brows. "Donald, would you like to take a drive?" Not waiting, Spencer ushered Donald to the car. Over his shoulder, he spoke, "See you later, Ken. If you need anything, I'm staying at Old Sam's place. Oh, Eurlene arrived and is here for a visit too. She's already redecorating." The car doors closed, and Spencer looked just for a moment at Donald and sped away.

"Where we going, ole boy?"

He snorted. "To the church."

Donald warned. "You're going to enter a hornet's nest."

"Why's that, Donald?"

"Kate and Louise are upholstering seats. I left when the Lady Ma Mere arrived."

Two quick weeks passed. Sylvia had enjoyed her time in the big city where she, J. J., and Mariah attended flashy shows and fine dinners. Everyone was sickeningly polite, but Sylvia felt some stress in her daughter, especially when J. J. walked into the room.

Sylvia asked Mariah, "Have you fallen out of love with J. J.?"

Mariah said, "Oh no, Mother! Quite the opposite. Only J. J. doesn't mention our getting married anymore. I think he's bored with courting me. You know how the public is so demanding. There are photos of him in the paper with a different girl at a different place every week. I know Eurlene's behind his grooming. However, he has become secretive, lately." Mariah stomped around the kitchen, and the marble floor carried the echoes of her steps.

Sylvia slid an arm around her daughter. "You're showing green, my dear, and it's not a good color on you. Listen to Mother. You're not due at work today, so let's just you and I go window-shopping." Sylvia waited and hunched her shoulders. "Please?"

A smile touched Mariah's full lips. "Give me a minute to change, and we'll go."

Sylvia let out a deep breath. "This assignment is more difficult than I thought. Just maybe we'll find a dress."

"Mom, I'm ready."

"Let's walk. I know it is coat-and-boot weather outside, but the sky is beautiful, bright, and the huge fluffy snowflakes floating are breathtaking. It prompts people's moods in shopping. And I could use a better dress, one for formal wear. Where are the best shops?"

Sylvia grabbed her purse and hooked her arm in Mariah's.

"We're headed there. It's just a few more blocks down the street, and the store serves the best hot tea. Great, I say, for a day like this."

"Wonderful." Another smile escaped, and Sylvia quietly hummed a tune.

"Look, Mariah, wedding dresses and veils." Sylvia nudged Mariah into the store. "What does it hurt one to look and wish?"

"Mother, I said J. J. is not that interested anymore."

" Well are you and he still having date nights? What about flirting with him?"

Mariah held up her arms. Sylvia's eyes followed. A V-neck, silken white wedding dress was displayed on a rack by itself. It was narrowed at the waist and appeared to have a semifull skirt.

"Mariah, look, the dress! It's so you. Why not try it on? Oh my!" Sylvia clasped her hands. "See, there is a perfect tiara with a long satin or silk veil. It would trail the length of the wedding dress." Not waiting, Sylvia reached for the head dressing and clapped her hands in the air for service.

Mariah shook her head all the way to the dressing room. When she stepped from the room, her face glowed, and she couldn't keep from smiling. "Mother, did you know that this dress was ordered from overseas, but the bride ordering it eloped."

"Her misfortune, my dear. It fits you like a glove, and nothing would need to be done. Try on the veil."

Mariah stooped. The attendant pulled Mariah's hair back in a bun and placed the tiara above. Then the attendant lifted and fluffed the tooling, straightening out the length.

Mariah stood. "Mother?"

Sylvia's mouth gaped, and tears formed in her eyes. She pulled a hankie from her sleeve. "You're absolutely beautiful. Just breathtaking." She glanced at the attendant. "We'll take the dress and veil." Sylvia stood and snapped her fingers. "I don't need to know the cost. Here's the address I want this delivered to, and here's my charge."

"Mariah, find me a dress!" she snapped.

Mariah marched in double time and strained to see farther into the store where a sign was posted: "Rack One-of-a-Kind." She thumbed through and selected a light blue sweetheart dress with matching jacket and padded shoulders. She spotted a jeweled evergreen dress and a red velvet long-sleeved dress, which had a V-neck. Mariah brought them all to a dressing room and motioned for her mother.

"Which is your favorite?" She stood with the light blue one on but eyed the red one. She wasn't tempted with the green or the blue. She reached for the red dress and waited on Mariah's treasured answer.

"Mom, you would look fabulous. With it being winter and all, well, that's my choice."

"Mine too. Do you think we can find shoes to match?" Sylvia was lost in the moment. Sylvia changed and called the attendant. "We need shoes."

The attendant scurried, carrying shoes and handbags for both ladies. Mariah tried on five or six pairs. She settled on a white beaded slingback pair.

Sylvia tried on all that were brought to her, but she didn't like any of the selections. She graciously thanked the women, paid for Mariah's, and headed out the door when Mariah stopped.

Sylvia almost tripped and held her hand out to catch her fall. "What's wrong?"

"Look. There in the window is exactly the pair you need, Mother." Mariah pointed to the attendant, and she quickly brought the shoes. There were rhinestones around the back, and they were the perfect shade of red.

The lady handed down two matching handbags, one in white and the other in red. Sylvia squealed. "They're beautiful. We'll take them. Here, take this package and send everything to the address I provided you with earlier."

She waltzed to the lingerie department with her happiness soaring and sorted through the finer undergarments and nightgowns. She held up different ones for Mariah to give her opinion. Some were very daring, some were rich in color, but then the silk gowns were worth handling. Mariah nodded as her mother selected two different sets in white for her. One was trimmed in dainty beadwork, and the other was in fluffy feathers. Both came with matching robes.

Mariah held up the cutesy sleepers. "I'm buying these, Mother. Aren't they feminine?"

Sylvia added a few undergarments to the pile. "And these, miss, send all to the same address."

"Mother, did you get a set?"

Sylvia felt the heat in her face rise. "Didn't you say I looked good in red?" Then she covered her mouth, trying to suppress a giggle.

They went into several more stores and bumped into J. J. He tipped his hat and pulled his coat collar up.

"J. J., what brings you in this neighborhood?"

"Well, I have a gala ball to attend, and I was looking for a new tuxedo. I called your place, Mariah." His blue eyes appeared to be pleading. "I would like for you to attend the ball with me."

Sylvia said, "J. J., what day and time?"

He placed a finger inside his collar, loosening it. Still gazing into Mariah's hazel eyes, he said, "The event is Saturday. I was just informed by Eurlene's phone call. Want to shop with me?" He raised an eyebrow.

Sylvia nudged Mariah. "Sure, we would love to, and let's eat out afterward."

He smiled and offered both his arms for the ladies to hold. They strolled into the men's formal wear and were shown a sitting area. Sylvia noticed how dark the wood trim and the store décor were compared to the ladies' stores. The management served coffee while J. J. slipped into the dressing room. He was not shy and modeled suit after suit.

Mariah's hands went to her mouth when J. J. stepped out in a long-tailed black coat, a shiny cummerbund, and tailored slacks. He added a silver watch pendant, cuff links, and a black-on-black bow tie, and topped everything with a hat, gloves, and a cane. His socks were ribbed silk, and his shoe selection was shiny black leather.

His lips crinkled at the sides as he bowed for Mariah's attention. "How do I look?"

Mariah glanced through her long eyelashes at her mother and took a sip of coffee. "You are very debonair." And she blurted out, "I would be honored to attend the gala ball with you." Her hazel eyes widened, and her hands flew to her mouth.

Sylvia folded her hands and nodded to J. J.

"Thank you, Mariah, for showing your interest in being my date. What color of flowers would you like to wear?"

"Surprise me, J. J. You have exquisite taste." Mariah batted her eyes.

J. J.'s bluish eyes deepened to blue green until they appeared as a deep pool. He bowed again, left, dressed into his street clothes, and signed for his purchase.

As they were almost out the door, Sylvia motioned for them to go across the street to the diner and that she would join them.

J. J. began to give his appeal on staying, but Sylvia would not hear any part of it. He paused, looking puzzled, but Mariah took his hand and smiled, leading the way across the street.

Sylvia addressed the salesman and swore him to secrecy. She ordered an outfit like the one J. J. had tried on with all the bells and whistles to be sent at the bed-and-breakfast in Mississippi. She also selected Donald, Ken, and Jon a new tux, shirt, the works. Sylvia caught the corner light; she huffed and puffed, fighting the winds. She clutched her coat closer. J. J. rose, met her, and helped her be seated.

At the restaurant, they made small talk and enjoyed their time together. J. J. paid for the meal, leaving a generous tip, and flagged them a cab. He placed an arm around Mariah. She touched his cheek and batted her eyes.

16

J. J. wiggled his foot while standing with the cabbie. He waited for the ladies to be seated. He slid in and sat beside Mariah. The cabbie closed the door.

The ride was bumpy but not far, although the weather appeared to be turning questionable. Again, he stepped out and waited for the ladies. He paid the fare and saluted the cabbie.

"Care to come up and have some hot chocolate?"

"Mariah, do you have marshmallows?"

She batted her eyes again. "Certainly, what would a hot chocolate be without them?"

J. J. shucked off his coat, placing it over his arm, and swung an arm around Mariah. "Are you cold, sweetheart? I feel you trembling."

She jerkily gave him her key. The door opened, and Mariah padded along the chairs until she sat down. Sylvia knew Cupid was with them, so she smoothly slid into the kitchen and began making the cocoa. "Where are the marshmallows? Anyone?"

She glanced in the doorway at J. J. and then at Mariah. He had embraced Mariah, and she was holding him back. Sylvia smiled and shook her head. She thought about the women's agreement about the two needing to be married and the sooner the better.

The week passed, and the snow lifted as Sylvia said her good-byes and left for Mississippi, leaving Mariah behind. Unbeknownst to Mariah, it was to join Kate and the Lady Ma Mere. She wanted to share her news, and she wanted in on the gossip about their adventures.

Sylvia took a cab and stopped first at the church. The winds blew and felt like ice hitting her face. "Hello, Kate, Louise." She walked further in and saw the beautiful covered pews. "Ladies, this is beautiful work."

Louise nodded. "When did you arrive and how is Mariah? Is she here?"

Kate said, "Thanks for the warning of things arriving. You have a ton of packages in the room. Did you buy out the stores?" She reached for Sylvia and gave her a welcoming hug. "Was it hard being with your daughter and J. J.?"

"Well, let's say it wasn't the easiest. Mariah can be something else sometimes, but I do know we are right to plan their wedding. They are like checkmate in chess." Sylvia turned as the ladies gathered their things. "Would you want to ride with me to the bed-and-breakfast?"

Both ladies answered yes.

The taxi was already filled with boxes and packages when suddenly a shrill Lady Ma Mere appeared and crammed herself into the seat, The four ladies carried their packages into their rooms. Louise shared a room with Kate.

Louise showed Sylvia the packages. They worked together and unpacked and hung everything up in the closet. Sylvia then made a phone call to Jon, but the answering machine directed her call to Ken's. She complained, "What is going on, and why would Jon be there?"

Later, the four ladies met at the local restaurant next door. Each one spoke at the same time. They laughed. Lady Ma Mere tapped her water glass. "Kate, Louise, please give us an update concerning the church pews."

Kate squeezed Louise's swollen and pricked hand. "We have finished upholstering all the seats and benches. Quite frankly, our fingers will never be the same."

Lady Ma Mere wiggled her index finger. She turned her attention toward Sylvia. "Now, I know we are all dying to hear about the lovebirds." She pouted. "And why is Mariah not here, daughter?"

Sylvia set her water glass down. "First, I understand Jon is here at Ken's place. Pray tell me, does anyone know anything about that?" She looked around. Kate's mouth went open, but no one said a word. Sylvia took another sip. "Both Mariah and J. J.'s wedding attire is here." She beamed. "They are playing cat and mouse with each other, but one can see the love sparks fly. My mission is complete. However, we still need to get them here and obtain a marriage license."

Lady Ma Mere held her cup up for more tea. She said, "Spencer has agreed for the usage of Old Sam's place. He has told Eurlene by now for she was headed to the newly purchased surprise farm." Lady Ma Mere crossed her arms.

Louise asked, "Who's not accounted for, and what is our next plan of action? Oh, Jud's on his way here to collect the check from the sale of Sara's business."

Lady Ma Mere's lips went thin, and through gritted teeth, she said, "We need Karen and the twins here. What about Claudia and Jack? You know that Mariah, unlikely as it seems, is really close to her." She clucked.

Sylvia gestured with her hand. "Of course, we need Dad. What's our plan? Don't forget. We need Eurlene in on this. She can summon J. J!"

Sylvia cleared her throat and said, "For the record, his clothes are here. Tuxedo, I mean. Mother Ma Mere? You need to call a meeting to include Sam, Ken, Sara, and Miechael to inform them about this wedding."

Kate choked. "I'll call Karen and let her know about the planned wedding and ask her to come and bring the twins. Also, to have Karen inform Miss Phyler that she needs to cover longer for her employer, Jud, than planned."

"Kate, will you speak with Donald tonight? Ask him to bring Jon with him."

Lady Ma Mere stood up. "I understand another trip to see Eurlene and Spencer is in store, but all things considered, I think Eurlene will be ready for the challenge."

"How are we going to get the bride-to-be and the groom-to-be here and on board with our plans?" Sylvia stretched her hands outward.

Silence settled in. A chair squeaked. Lady Ma Mere cleared her throat. "I'll have Eurlene come up with an excuse for J. J. to come here. She can have Tom cover the New York bank for a few days longer, I'm sure. And I'll call the Duke. He will escort Mariah here. She won't turn him down." Lady Ma Mere looked over her shoulder. "Sylvia, are the invitations completed? Their wedding is on Christmas Eve. Make sure you post them. My address book is in the top of my suitcase."

"Mother, should we meet at Ken's tonight for an intervention meeting?"

"Louise, Kate, will you be in charge of dinner tonight? I'll ask Spencer and Eurlene to join us. We must stand firm." Lady Ma Mere hunched her shoulders.

Kate and Louise stared at each other. "Isn't that Donald?" Kate flagged him over and ordered coffee for her husband. The surprise wedding was explained, and they waited for Donald to say something, but instead he just laughed till tears came. "A shotgun wedding, love it."

A cab pulled up and out stepped Jon. Louise stood up and motioned to him to join them. She asked the server to bring another chair and to pour him a cup of coffee.

"Where's Sylvia? I heard she was here."

Sylvia appeared and flashed a smile. They hugged and then sat down. "I'll have coffee, please."

Kate's eyes narrowed as Sylvia announced, "All of us are due at Ken's and Sara's for dinner. Louise and I are in charge."

Donald quickly filled Jon in on the shotgun wedding, and he started laughing. Sylvia placed her hand on Jon's and asked, "Will you help me fill in the time and date and help me with addressing the invitation envelopes? Oh, Louise, Sara needs you to call Claudia or have Ken call."

Louise sighed. "I may need something stronger than tea." She reached out both of her hands, and each person joined hands with each other, making a circle. They each took a moment of silence before continuing with the massive plan.

Kate called the bed-and-breakfast and added another suite.

The air began to whip, and the wind howled. The lights flickered off and on. Louise and Kate were busy cooking. Sara ventured into the kitchen and picked up a stirring spoon. Kate pulled out a chair and motioned to her to sit. Louise brought a bowl of potatoes and a peeler, pointed to Sara, and took the spoon. "Thank you for volunteering." Louise touched Sara's shoulder. "Have you or Ken called Claudia and Jack inviting them to Mariah's and J. J.'s wedding? It's for next week. But maybe you can use another reason for their coming so they don't give the surprise away. You know sweet Claudia."

Sara held the peeler and a spud, but her mouth gaped. She said, "Wedding." Just then, the baby kicked, and the ladies swooned.

Ken, unknown to the women, was standing in the kitchen's doorway. He paused. "Is J. J. and my sister finally getting married? Well, hurray, J. J. finally worked up the nerve to ask and move forward." He tossed his hat in the air.

Louise touched his arm. "Sorry, Ken, but Mariah and J. J. have been so busy with their careers and thoughts of a wedding hadn't even surfaced so…"

Kate smiled and said, "While Donald and I were on the cruise with the Lady and Duke Ma Mere, we talked about the young ones' wedding a lot. Being that the Lady and the Duke Ma Mere are scheduled to travel all next year, we formed a plan for Mariah and J. J."

Ken stepped back, and Donald and Sam sat down. "What?"

Jon spoke up. "Kate, Louise, and the Lady Ma Mere have rented the church in town. Kate and Louise upholstered all the pews and benches." Turning to the ladies, he continued. "I might add, ladies, beautiful work." Again, he locked eyes with Ken. "So, son, you know Spencer bought Old Sam's place."

"Did I hear my name?" Spencer entered the room.

The large kitchen appeared smaller with Eurlene and Spencer looped arm in arm. Lady Ma Mere stood clutching her coat and smiling like a Cheshire cat.

Jon ventured again. "Spencer, you did hear your name in connection with buying Sam's place."

Lady Ma Mere butted in. "The reception will be at Eurlene and Spencer's place. They graciously invited us to have the party there."

Ken let out a deep breath and looked at Sara. She shrugged her shoulders but broke into a smile. "How are you getting J. J. here? And what about Mariah?"

Eurlene said, "Ken, it's quite simple. Tom is staying on to cover the bank. And he was instructed to give J. J. a message, saying he's to be on such and such a flight and what day per his sister Eurlene. I'm taking no calls from him." She turned, and Spencer brought her closer to him.

"Well, if that doesn't beat all. He's being railroaded. It serves him right for dragging his feet. I'm on board. What about Mariah? Now that will be tricky."

"Really?" Lady Ma Mere snorted. "The duke was delighted in his part. He's escorting Mariah here. For Christmas week."

Sara said, "Ken, isn't the new foal ready? As it was promised to Claudia, perhaps Claudia and Jack could come with intentions of picking up the colt."

Ken's eyes twinkled. "You are like a spider. The webs you weave. They don't stand a chance." They laughed.

"Ken and Sara, that leaves you two to let Miechael know he's getting a new stepfather and to ask him if he'll participate in the wedding."

The next few days whirled by, and the newscaster promised it would be a cold, blustery few days. The fact that the sun was fully shining and the clouds were drifting white and feathery gave the illusion that it was warmer than it really was.

The duke privately consulted with Mariah about spending Christmas in Mississippi with her brother, family, and son. On the plane, the Duke said, "You are also finally marrying that Joshua Brown fellow. This wedding is long over due!" He in silence looked out the airplane window.

Mariah wanted to scream but bit her lip. She said, "What do you mean I'm getting married? I don't think so!" She crossed her arms and shrillingly laughed. Moments later, Mariah steamingly said, "I don't even have a dress. Duke, you know it takes weeks to plan a wedding!" She scooted back in her seat and lowly said, "Hum, wedding indeed."

Duke straightened and glared down at Mariah. "You, my dear, are not to worry your pretty little head." He patted her hand. "Every thing has been arranged for this wedding to Joshua Brown." He slightly turned, adding, "Joshua Brown is a good man!" He air kissed Mariah's cheek. Duke reached into his jacket pocket and said, "Mariah, here is a gift from your husband to be."

She hurriedly opened the wrapped package. There in the red velvet box was a handmade platinum and white gold locked. She fingered the letter etching M. Opening the locket, Mariah saw a picture of J. J. and her. She remembered the photo was taken at Eurelene's wedding. Her tearful eyes move to the photo beside.

It was of her son and J. J. Mariah drew the lock to her chest. In a whisper, she said, "Duke, will you close the catch on my locket." He slipped the necklace around her neck. Her lips were quivering.

Eurlene had a private meeting with J. J. No one knew what was spoken, but she, Spencer, Miechael, and J. J. picked up his clothing from Sylvia's room the day before Mariah arrived.

That night alone in his sister's home, J. J. paced the floor and said, "I'm getting married, married, tomorrow. Wow!" He swiveled on his shoe heel. "I didn't think this day would ever get here with Mariah's change of moods. She said yes. I'm glad she… what if she didn't go along with the plan? And I can't get in touch with her because Eurlene demanded me not to make contact in anyway, shape, or form with Mariah." J. J. blotted his brow.

The big day was under way. Limousines were stationed for standby. A red carpet was laid on the walkway for Mariah. The trumpet players were lined and poised for instant playing. The last poinsettias were placed down both sides of the church aisles. Jon, her adoptive father, was dressed in a gray long-tailed tux. He stepped from the vehicle and opened the door for a happy, but subdued, Mariah. He had a sweet smile, and he slightly bowed and tipped his hat. Mariah accepted his arm, and for a moment, they locked eyes. Together, they climbed the covered steps leading them toward the aisle and the front, where J. J. and his groomsmen stood.

On the platform stood two trumpet players; they had been assigned for Mariah's entrance announcement. The organ pedal was held to increase note vibration, quieting the crowd. The piano player starkly fingered the keys, and the wedding march began. The people were gestured and then motioned to rise. The soldiers stood at attention and pointed their swords. Mariah and her dad took a step. But at the doorway, Claudia muscled in and dragged Jack.

Jon paused. He patted Mariah's hand and gave it a little squeeze. Mariah bit her lip to suppress a giggle. She gave Claudia an air kiss. The piano player struck the chord again. Jon moved forward. Mariah's veil flowed airy and motionless and briefly touched the floor. Each step was accentuated, defining the march. Mariah's hazel eyes searched the front of the church and locked eyes with her husband-to-be. She glanced at Miechael and noticed that his dark eyes were moist. It captured her heart. She trembled and smiled. Mariah clutched her bridal bouquet of long-stemmed red and yellow roses and held on to her father's hand.

Mariah viewed each pew and saw that they were wrapped in a broad white satin ribbon. Candles were in every window in groups of three. The matron of honor, Eurlene, held a bouquet with a scented candle woven into it. Candles were in golden holders at the front of the church, and poinsettias were on the platform.

The anticipating groom shifted from foot to foot. He was wearing a single red rose that was laced in gold and arranged on his black long-tailed coat.

Mariah admired how fashionable J. J. looked with his charcoal gray trousers. She observed the groomsman—her son, Miechael—and saw that he wore a single rose boutonniere of yellow entwined with red.

As Jon and Mariah approached the front, Miechael stepped forward, bowed, took his mother's hand, and linked it with J. J.'s. The three approached the altar, and the minister began.

Mariah's dress swished, and she appeared like a bell in the woven pearl semicircle skirt. Her V-neck and tightly laced bodice only enhanced her dainty appearance. For something old, she wore pearls given to her from the Lady Ma Mere; and for something new, she wore pearl droplet earrings from her mother, Sylvia. She smiled, knowing her blue was hidden for the time being. She was thrilled for her nine-inch heels, but J. J. with his broad shoulders towered yet a few inches above her. His red snappy hair against her alluring European locks of black only emphasized their differences but totally complemented them.

The nuptial vows the minister gave were solemn and eloquent. The instruments on cue quieted. The soldiers stood in place A dropped pin could have been heard. The minister announced the kiss of the son to his mother. It was an added ritual, and a formal handshake and a bow was given to his new stepfather. Miechael nodded to his mother and stepped to the side, watching as the minister said to J. J., "You may kiss your bride."

It appeared a lengthy time during the kiss, but from the crowd, a shrill whistle and a voice traveled like a sonic boom. "J. J. you're now wearing a ball and chain."

The room went stonily silent for a few seconds, and then there was a throwing of hats, loud hoots and hollers, whistles, and a standing ovation. It didn't matter that there was royalty.

The minister raised his arms and announced, "Meet, for the first time, Mr. and Mrs. Joshua Jimso Brown. Reception follows." Nodding his head in Spencer's direction, he said, "It's at Old Sam's place." He was given a note. "Bring your appetites."

The couple was ushered to a parked limousine. J. J. kissed Mariah before she was seated, and the wild birdseed and rice were still settling. The Ma Meres and the older News couple joined in letting the doves loose. The crowd clapped again. J. J. helped Mariah with her dress and veil. He arose from his haunches and faced Miechael. J. J. motioned then asked, "Coming, sport?"

Kate peeked at Louise. She glanced at Eurlene and eyed the friends she had come so dearly to love. The ladies all held their handkerchiefs, dabbing gingerly under their eyes.

Claudia made her way through the crowd and slapped the Lady Ma Mere on the back. "Ain't that beautiful what J. J. did? He's a godsend, that one is." She sniffed and adjusted her floppy hat. Claudia waved to Jack, and he came alongside as she was shaking the Duke's hand, who was thanking them for the invitation to their granddaughter's wedding.

An announcement was made: "Limousines are waiting for those wanting a ride to the reception."

Spencer and Eurlene hurried to their home to be on site for the arriving guests. They found Kate and Louise already there, busily warming and handling the food. Donald and Sam were taking orders and carrying the food to their destinations. Donald lit the candles under the warming pans and continued in aiding Sam to bring food to the tables.

Ken arranged three long tables in the dining room and had Eurlene store her rustic table setting during the wedding reception.

Written on an artistic blackboard was the menu.

> Choice: roast beef, southern fried chicken, or maple cured ham
> Potato dishes: mashed, baked, or augratin
> Vegetables: peas, green beans, or corn
> Freshly tossed salad
> Drinks: coffee or mint chocolate iced tea made by Karen Day

17

The ladies talked as they worked on packing the sale items of Sara's purse business. Eurlene learned that her baby brother had formed an association of Brown and Brown's and bought Sara's purse business. Of course, Eurlene bragged about his professional manners and pointed a finger at him.

J. J. carried his and Mariah's glasses and refilled them with iced tea. Mariah could only watch him for his muscles rippled under his tux coat. There was innocence in his smile, and the corners of his eyes lifted. She held her breath after seeing his five-o'clock shadow peeking. She whispered, "He's so ruggedly handsome." Mariah stepped beside him, and their energy played off each other.

Everyone seemed to mingle with ease with the variety and different cultures represented. Even when Claudia took her hands and embraced J. J.'s face, making him pucker up, Mariah laughed. She took her strange friend's hand to her bosom, patted it, and gave it a squeeze. She said, "Claudia, how are you and Jack doing?"

Claudia's eyes widened. "Me and Jack are like glue. He has started a Wednesday night Bible study at the house, and people are flocking in. He hit it up good with my other right-hand man, and my Jack also helps out now with the horses. Just look at him."

She sighed. "I'm blessed and so lucky. He's everything to me. Oh, this is about you and your hunk." She hugged Mariah in a bear hug. She coughed but smiled genuinely.

Duke Ma Mere left J. J. and Mariah's side. He approached Karen, smiling. She nodded. He said, "I see the twins are having fun." He looked toward them. "I think Luci may have a little crush on Timmy."

Karen chuckled. "You're probably right. Maybe it's both ways."

"Karen, I see telltale signs of swelling. What does the doctor say? And how are you and the baby really doing?"

Karen saw genuineness in the Duke Ma Mere's eyes. "Sir, I'm not in much pain, but the amount of water held is discouraging."

Duke Ma Mere stepped to the side and cupped a hand as he whispered, "It's still only one, isn't it?"

Karen looked at the crinkles by the man's dark eyes then said, "The doctor has ordered another ultrasound when we return home. He is either wrong on the due date, or I'm packing more than one. I was tired in the beginning, but lately, I am having all kinds of energy."

He placed a hand on her shoulder. "Rest while you can. If this one takes after you, it will be a pistol." He shook with laughter while holding his belly.

Karen rolled her blue eyes.

Jud stepped forward. "Darling, how can you keep looking so lovely and ageless? You're not overdoing yourself, are you?" He lifted his eyebrow.

She took his offered hand and let him lead. Spencer tapped Jud on the shoulder and glanced around. "Karen, are you up to a few dance steps around the room?"

Jud's smile reached his green smoldering eyes. "Only at arm's length. Remember that she goes home with Spencer." He bowed and stepped aside.

Karen blushed a bright pink while taking Spencer's arm.

Eurlene waltzed over and reached for Jud's hand. He breathed deeply as he posed. Eurlene's striking looks still made people stop and gawk. Her fiery red hair bounced, and her body-hugging sheath dress warmed a body up.

Karen thanked Spencer and did a sprint to gain Jud's arm. She batted her lashes, hoping to make her blue eyes inviting. Jud bowed, dropped his arms from Eurlene, and encircled Karen in his. He bent and lingered with a kiss. Karen felt his strength and heat.

Eurlene gave a throaty laugh as she snagged Spencer. He placed his hand on her back, led her to the dance area to dance to a few slow songs, and then walked her to the sofa. Sylvia stopped by with Jon and graciously thanked them for opening their home and for being hosts to the reception.

Spencer stood and shook hands with Jon. "Our pleasure." His eyes swept over Eurlene's face with tenderness. Eurlene stood and linked her arm in Spencer's, and they locked eyes.

Miechael tapped on a glass while standing on an ottoman. "Ladies and gentlemen, may I have your attention?" He glanced over the crowd and motioned J. J. and his mother to come up front. "To the newlyweds, my mother, Mariah, and my new father, Joshua. May they always be as happy as they are this moment." He held his iced tea up. "Hear, hear!"

J. J. was passed the microphone. Holding hands with his bride, he lovingly looked at Miechael. "Folks, I've been blessed two times over. And thank you for knowing what was best for Mariah and me, for us."

The crowd cheered and clapped. Claudia and Jack slipped into their coats. Claudia whistled and motioned for Ken. "Want to help load the foal? Jack and I are heading out. Time to be getting home." She took Jack's hand and lifted them together in the air. "Bye, you all. J. J., you be good to Mariah. You two come and visit us, ya hear? See real country."

Jon and Sylvia made their way over to the Ma Meres and bade them good night and good-bye. Sara and the boys, including Miechael, hitched a ride with Ken's mom and dad to the house.

Eurlene jumped when the phone rang. "Hello, Tom. To what do I owe the pleasure of your call? Is there anything wrong at the bank?"

"No. No, Eurlene.

Eurlene said, "Too much noise going on in here. Hold please. All right go ahead."

Tom let out a breath and said, "Miss Phyler wouldn't take a vacation, but she did agree to handle the bank's affairs in New York. Miss Phyler said she must keep busy. Although she insists you call in bright and early Monday morning to report to her and confirm your schedule and plans. However, Eurlene, I did receive a disturbing phone call from Mr. Albert Rich. He's Red Nolan Spencer's attorney. Red Nolan Spencer is uncle to Spencer."

"Do you need to speak with Spencer?"

"No. You'll do just fine." He puffed. "Mr. Rich said he's sorry to report that there had been an accident claiming the lives of Spencer's uncle and his wife. It was an automobile crash, and the accident snuffed out their lives instantly. The car slid, the uncle lost control on an icy patch, and the car hit a tree. They were dead on impact. His attorney went on to say that they left two surviving children—a girl named Abigail, aged ten, and a baby boy named Hunter, aged three months. Mr. Red Nolan Spencer named you and Spencer as the children's guardians. You need to call this number, 212-554-3321. He's expecting to hear from you tonight to make arrangements and transport the children. Again, Eurlene, I'm sorry for your and Spencer's loss." Tom let out a deep breath. "Tell Jud that Dora and I will be at the bed-and-breakfast when they get home. Okay?"

Only a low, husky voice was audible. "Tom, thanks for all your help at the bank and for forwarding this information. Be in touch, please."

Spencer saw Eurlene flop down, and she appeared ghostly. "Darling?" He held her, and she shook. He closed the door to their room for privacy. "What's wrong?"

She pushed him to sit in the bucket-style chair. Eurlene sat on his lap. She explained the phone conversation she had with Tom and handed him the phone number. Spencer's mouth gaped. "Guardians? My uncle and aunt are dead? I haven't seen Uncle Red Nolan Spencer in quite a while. Matter of fact, it was a week before we left for Spain, and when I did, he seemed so happy." As if Spencer was already recovered from the shocking words, he poked her to get up. He resumed business mode. "Eurlene, we'll have Mariah and J. J. stay here. They can keep an eye on things and get our place back in order." He raised an eyebrow and placed his hand on her thigh. "Amongst other things."

"Oh, Spencer, I love you."

He made the call then Spencer hailed J. J. and Mariah to the room. "You kids will stay here for your honeymoon. You'll have peace and quiet after you see that everything is put back in its place. The loan furniture is to be taken down, and the storage pieces are to be set in place."

Eurlene touched Mariah's hand. "We've an emergency needing our immediate attention. We are leaving yet tonight for Texas. Take and use the spare room. It's large in size, and you should be quite comfortable. My Bentley is being delivered here in the next day or two. Please inspect it and make sure it's fine. Be careful, but you can drive it, J. J. No nonsense out of you, and do use both hands on the wheel. Should Miss Phyler call about bank business, please forward her to me." As an afterthought, she added, "She's another story all of itself. Don't even ask."

Mariah sounded humbled. "Oh, Eurlene, thank you for the use of Old Sam's place. Your design is so tasteful and is awesome. We'll be careful with everything." She hugged Eurlene and gave her a kiss on her cheek. "Be careful driving and call us. Again, thank you for your hospitality."

"Eurlene, pack light," Spencer said. "If we need anything, we'll purchase it there. Meet me in the truck in fifteen minutes. I've made flight arrangements."

"Spencer, are you not driving to Texas?"

Eurlene shuddered and packed, not folding a thing. She threw his stuff in one case and hers in another. She picked up her smallest makeup case and, as an afterthought, placed some sleepwear items in it. She dialed Ken's number and was grateful that he answered the phone. "Ken?"

"Yes, Eurlene?"

"Ken, Spencer and I have been called out of town. His uncle and aunt were in a fatal car accident and left two children. It's mind-boggling. But Mariah and J. J. will be staying here at our place. Oh, and Mariah wants you to say hi to Miechael." Eurlene handed Mariah the phone.

"Hello, Miechael. Thanks for the cheer tonight." She giggled. "We're not far away. We're staying at Old Sam's place if you need us."

"Mom, will J. J. adopt me? It's my wish that he does."

"Son, we'll talk about this important matter. We love you."

"Mom, I overheard Uncle Ken talking with Eurlene. Are they going to raise the two orphaned children?"

"Shush. Leave all those details to the adults."

"Mom, the girl is my age. She must feel all alone."

"We'll know more after they call or come home. Until then, you pray for the two children and their loss. Stay good for your Uncle Ken. Night, sweetheart." The phone clicked and left only a buzzing sound.

J. J. touched her cheek and softly said, "Mariah, are you all right? What did the little tyke ask you?"

Mariah twisted her head and set her hand on the nook. "He wants you to adopt him. He wants a real dad. I wasn't expecting him to ask."

"How do you feel being his mother?"

"What if our marriage doesn't last?" She locked eyes with J. J.

Hands on hips, he asked, "Where do you think I'm going? I wouldn't marry if I were uncertain at all. Do you think I'm not good enough to be his father?"

Mariah saw his blue eyes narrow with intensity. He paced the floor, and she knew they needed to get back to their guests. She reached his shoulder. "Let's see to our guests, and we'll talk about this later."

Mariah turned. J. J. grabbed her arm. She whirled into his body. "We'll talk now." He bent and kissed her. She responded, and they lingered.

Jud called out, "J. J., Mariah, we're leaving."

J. J. buttoned his shirt, and Mariah slicked back her hair. J. J. approached Jud. "Thanks for coming and helping me in obtaining the new business. Will you help me with the Brown and Brown's business plans? Mariah and I will be staying and minding the house for Spencer and Eurlene. They left on an emergency. Something to do with his family—uncle and aunt's death, children left."

"I know," Jud answered. "Eurlene took me aside and spoke about Spencer's emergency. She also stated my father and his wife were headed to our bed-and-breakfast place. But, J. J., thank you." Jud placed a hand in his pocket, looked in Mariah's direction, and said, "Your challenges have just begun." He chuckled. "Now about the Brown business, let me know when you're ready to talk."

Mariah latched on to Jud's arm and walked beside Karen, Luke, Luci, Donald, Kate, Sam, and Louise toward the door. Each wormed their way into their coats, hats, boots, and gloves. As the door opened, a gust of wind blew in sheets of the newly fallen snow. The adults hugged Mariah and then J. J. and said their congratulations and their good-byes once again before rushing to the waiting limo. Donald helped his wife, Kate, and Sam helped Louise. Jud, with his arm around Karen, carefully reached for her puffy hand.

He gave the limo driver directions to Ken's house. It was a crazy ride. Jud offered to stay with Karen in the limo while the other couples went into Ken's house to retrieve their luggage. The foursomes were awaiting their travel adventure. They agreed to a much-needed vacation, so they arranged for a long cruise, with their destination the Caribbean Islands.

Karen asked Jud to go on and give their farewells for earlier she had slid trying to walk, even while holding on to him. She decided not to take another chance, so she stayed in the warm limo with the twins. Karen hollered, "Hurry if you can, honey. I'll read."

Louise, Kate, Sam, and Donald rushed to get back inside the limo. The twins became cranky, and Karen just wanted to lie down. She smiled as Jud reached her side. "Come, sweetheart, we're spending the night with Sara and Ken. I called and reached Dad, and they made it just fine to our place. He'll go into the bank and check out operations for me while Dora will get things ready for the bed-and-breakfast guests. Dad said for us to take our time in getting back, so I changed the flight arrangements. We leave in a couple of days, depending on the weather. Let's take time to relax, and Karen, you ladies can do some old-fashioned catching up. After all, it's Christmas time."

The snowflakes were cracker-size and steadily falling. Luke and Luci squealed. They took four or five steps, and Luci pulled Luke down, pointing. "Make snow angels with me."

Karen hung heavily on Jud's arm. The snow was ankle-deep and covered the ice from the previous freezing rain. Her heels were not a match for the outdoors. Jud wished he had on his hiking boots for it would have made walking easier. After much struggle, they reached the front porch. They gave a sigh of relief when Timmy and Matthew burst out the door, buttoning their coats and falling on the ground and trying to outdo each other. The four ganged up on Miechael and put snow down his shirt. He balled up the snow and threw it back, laughing.

Jud helped Karen inside, nodded to Sara, grabbed Ken, and pulled him out the door. Jud still had on his finest clothes, but the boy in him took over. They rolled and wrestled and then helped the children build an igloo and a fort. They made snowballs and decided after a no-win situation that both sides were to raise a white flag. The men, along with their children and Miechael, rolled snow to make a family of snowmen. Finally, they called it a night. Inside the house, the men and boys were directed to an outside porch to change clothes and dry off. Luci, however, was immediately ushered upstairs to a bathroom for a shower.

Sara and Karen still enjoyed the bedding down of their children and reading to them. This time, Miechael offered to stay with Timmy and Matthew, and they shared their room with Luke. Luci had her own room, thanks to Miechael.

The boys walked Luci to the bedroom and bid her good night. Timmy lingered. "Timmy, what are you still doing standing there?"

"Luci, I'm glad you're here. I had fun tonight." His face reddened. "I just want to say you were pretty at the wedding, and thank you for dancing with me." He leaned in and kissed her cheek.

Luci's light blue eyes widened. She closed the door and heard his footsteps leaving. She said her night prayers and then said, "What was that all about? Could he see I like him?" She bit her bottom lip as her mother entered the room and said, "Good night. Tomorrow morning is Christmas. We'll open packages after we get home with Tom and Dora. But for now, sleep, Luci."

18

Several days passed. The weather carried through its promise of being one of the worst winters Mississippians had ever seen or experienced. The airport canceled all flights in and out and finally closed the port. Phone lines had fallen to the ground from the pressure of snow, as did the electric lines and the cable lines. There were no lights or television. Candles were lit, and wood was carried in the house to maintain fires in the fireplaces. Also, the stove provided a place where kindling wood was added to heat the grate on the stove's surface.

In the evenings, Karen read. Even the adults paid attention as she pitched her weighted voice. She laughed in the funny parts and whispered when it seemed necessary. She appeared lost in the story.

Night snacks were given out, and then the children were dismissed. Sara and Ken tucked in Timmy, Matthew, and Miechael after they drank their last glasses of water for the night and said their prayers.

Luke hummed when slipping into his pajamas. And Luci asked her dad to tuck her in. When all the rituals were completed, both Karen and Jud backed from the rooms. They saw Luci fast asleep, and then they glanced in on the boys. Luke always had a smile on his face, but surprisingly, he too was sound asleep.

The men cooked. Jud urged Karen and Sara to rest. He heard their moans. And saw their puffy feet and the swollen legs. Pain was written on both women's faces. Yet they both rubbed their stomach and smiled.

Sara chuckled as she watched Karen's baby appear to stretch, pushing its little legs out and making a fisted hands movement as if flying. Then Sara's belly went completely to the left side and then to the right. Karen started laughing. "Your little girl will like roller coasters, I think."

Sara chuckled more. "You are probably right, my friend." Sara adjusted herself in the seat. "Karen, after you're home and visited with the doctor call me."

Karen blushed and nodded while rocking back and forth.

Sara said. "I will have my doctor's appointment by that time, and let's compare notes as to due dates."

"You're on." She giggled.

Ken stopped and frowned, but a slight trace of a smile curved his lips. He handed Jud a guitar and motioned him into the family room. Ken waited and saw Sara and Karen take another pillow and fluff the ones behind their backs. Jud pushed a footstool under their feet and handed them each a cover. Ken shook his head and began strumming. Jud joined. They did a few sweet and loving songs, watching each other's movements. And then they switched up the harmony.

The ladies clapped and swooned. Sara ventured to lift herself up and get dessert for them, but Jud held up his hand. "Sit and relax, Sara. We'll treat you both tonight." Jud headed for the kitchen, and Ken went to his rescue. The dishes clattered, and the glasses clinked. Out popped both Ken and Jud with their hands full, carrying pie and fresh iced tea.

Ken said, "Karen, when's your due date?"

Just then Sara let a moan slip.

Both men jumped and spoke at the same time. "What's wrong?"

Sara let out a breath. "The baby is kicking. Karen, remember when you were black and blue at your sides when carrying the twins?" Sara lifted her top slightly, and marks were there. "I must be carrying the baby sideways. Sometimes, it just plain hurts." She lightly rubbed her sides and sat back.

Karen patted her friend's arm. "I understand. Have you seen a diagram of the baby yet?"

The baby kicked again. Ken said, "Maybe she's swimming."

Laughter filled the room.

Jud noticed Karen had not sat comfortably for she kept shifting. He asked, "Want to lie down, sweetheart?"

She nodded. "I'm tired sorry, Sara I wish our nights of visiting could continue, but…It's been great seeing you both again and to share this special season. I've missed our visits."

Ken nodded. He rose to his feet and helped Sara into an upright stance. "We all need some rest." A grin spread on his face. "Wonder if the lovebirds are awake and how they're doing?"

Jud yawned and said, "Count me out for any horseplay. I think traveling and weddings have worn me out. Karen, come." His eyes were darkening. "I will walk you to the room." Over his shoulder, he asked, "Is it all right if I shower tonight? I know the water has been limited."

He picked up his and Karen's plates and glasses. Ken carried a tray and took over from there. Ken said, "Don't use all the hot water."

Jud said, "Cold is good enough for you, Ken."

The ladies giggled as the two bantered back and forth.

Karen, with feet apart, carried her shoes and clung to Jud's arm as he guided her up the stairs. She undressed and reached for her nightgown. She sat on the poster bed looking at her swollen feet and now ankles and her puffy hands. She placed two pillows at the end of the bed and swung her feet up. She felt the pain instantly as the fluid began to retract. Karen closed her eyes. She felt like an out-of-body experience was happening when Jud switched on the overhead light. It was so bright. She squinted and mumbled. "Do you mind?"

Jud swiveled around and dressed for bed. "Want me to take the other side?"

"Just turn out the light. You can see where I'm lying." She grunted. "I'll move over if you give me a foot rub."

Jud moved quickly and brought oils to the bed. He felt Karen relax as he finished the second foot. He bent and kissed her cheek. "I'll be right back." When he returned, she had moved over as promised. He slipped off his slippers and slid under the covers. She felt like toast and smelled fresh. Her hair was now down and had been brushed. A lemon fragrance wafted by. He placed his arm under her head, and she snuggled. The room was quiet, and Jud was slipping into a haze.

As Karen turned, the baby kicked. Instead of jumping, he placed his hand on her stomach. "Karen, I'm blessed and thank you."

He pulled the covers tighter, and she yawned. "If I turn over, will you rub my back?"

He moved his index finger in a swirl motion. She flipped over. He lightly rubbed her shoulders and tapered down her spine. She soon yawned again and reached for his hand. "Night, love, and thanks for the extra stay at Ken and Sara's."

He went to answer, but she batted her lashes closed. He bent, kissed her cheek, and settled on his back. He looked at the ceiling and watched the blades on the fan pass. He put his hands behind his head and woke to the squeak of Karen padding to the restroom. She hoisted herself on the bed. He moved closer to the edge. "Jud, I'm so miserable."

"What can I do to help?"

Karen placed a hand on his shoulder. "Remember how I got this way. Oh, the baby is awake. I can't relax."

"Would you like a hot tea?"

"I really would. Is it too much trouble?"

Jud was deprived of endless sleep, but Karen was his main focus. He patted her arm. "Darling, I'll be right back. Want some crackers or toast?"

"Uh huh." She stretched and yawned.

He removed his slippers and quietly placed her tea and toast on the side table. He lightly touched her cheek and walked around to the other side of the bed and once again slid in. He stayed on the edge so as not to wake the finally sleeping Karen.

The next morning, Ken and Jud dressed for the outdoors and waited on the kids to join them. Ken carried his old sled he used as a boy and the two others he had made for his two sons.

All the children squealed with happiness and excitement. The men pulled the children seated on the sleds. Miechael used Ken's sled. This was his first time playing in the snow. Jud saw apprehension and handed Ken the sled's rope he was pulling and went over to Miechael.

Jud pushed Miechael on the sled and then hopped on with him. Both were trying to guide the bars. The snow caused their faces to turn red, but the thrill of traveling through the air was unbelievable. Ken joined his boys, and Jud resumed playing with the twins. Walking up the hill, Miechael said, "Uncle Ken, ride with me, please?"

Ken's heart swelled. He gave a look to Jud and gave Miechael a push, and down the two traveled. You could hear the joy from the others as they watched the older boy have fun.

Jud saw his breath and noticed they were a long way from the house. He caught Ken's attention. "Isn't over the hill close to Old Sam's Place? Want to check on the newlyweds?"

"Yes. Maybe they'll give us some hot chocolate before heading back."

The boys heard and poked Luci. All seven were ready to fly down the hill. Timmy and Matthew on one sled watched Luke and Luci on another sled, and Miechael hopped on with Ken. Jud stepped to hop on the back of the twins when their sled let loose and took off. Timmy pushed off with his foot and went afterwards, the sled carrying himself and Matthew. They whizzed. Ken hurriedly jumped on. Miechael hollered to Jud, "Hurry down!"

Jud, not wanting to walk the distance, muttered, "On what? How am I going to make a sled?" Glancing around, he decided to take off his downy jacket and fixed it inside out. He sat down and pushed. It took three tries, some readjusting, and then, on his back with his feet in the air, he came down the long hill.

J. J., Ken, and the children at the bottom now watched as Jud's speed picked up. Looking like a white ball, Jud tried to yell, but his voice was lost in the wind. Mariah stepped outside and yelled, "J. J., are we in trouble? Is an avalanche coming?"

Ken burst out laughing, and so did the kids. Even Miechael laughed. Just then, the huge ball stopped. Jud slid into Ken and pushed him down, causing a domino effect. He was laughing and crying as he gathered himself up. "Anybody hurt?"

Ken, in between laughs, said, "I don't think so."

Both men were brushing themselves off.

Mariah stared with hands on hips. "What kind of leadership is this? Shame on you men."

Ken tackled his sister and rubbed her face in the snow. He stopped almost immediately for his stomach ached from laughing. J. J. helped Mariah up. His mouth gaped as Mariah reached with Miechael and gave J. J. a shove, snickering. J. J. tottered and slid. He tried to gain balance, but he landed on Mariah. Her wide hazel eyes bulged. Everyone, including Mariah and J. J., finally gave in to laughter.

The warmth from the fireplace felt good. Mariah asked J. J. to fix hot chocolate. She changed her clothes, only this time she changed into slacks and a sweater, still wearing nine-inch stilted-heel boots.

Later the boys, Luci, and the men's outerwear dried. The snow kept falling, and all former paths were covered. They had traveled for at least ten country miles. Mariah said, "Eurlene's Bentley is here. Would you want J. J. to take you home?"

Ken and Jud spoke in unison. "No.

J. J. said, "Old Sam has a tractor still in the barn, and there is also a wagon. It's not much, but we have some gas. Travel will be better than trying to walk."

All slid on their coats, boots, hats, and gloves and nodded yes in unison.

Mariah was standing in the doorway waving when J. J. pulled up in front of the house, saying, "Get shaking, Mariah. Grab your warmest coat. You're coming too."

She shook her shoulders while shimmying into her coat. She cheerfully yelled, "Just a minute."

Luci said, "Mariah, those heeled boots aren't going to help if we get stuck."

Jud and Ken nudged J. J., keeping him from laughing again.

Mariah tilted her head higher. "Luci, that's what the men are for. They're strong and pigheaded coming out in this weather."

Luci watched Mariah for the longest time and said, "Mariah, it's fun to play in the snow. You can make snow angels."

The boys joined in. "Snowballs fights, forts, igloos."

Miechael moved closer to his mother. "J. J., stop for a moment. Please."

He jumped from the wagon and reached for his mother's gloved hand. "Mother, step down. I'll help you."

"What?"

"Now mother."

The men observed Mariah as she stepped from the wagon. "What now, Miechael?"

"Look, Mother, lie down on the snow and move your hands up and down and move your feet in and out."

"Why would I want to do that?"

"Come, Mother! It's fun. See?"

Mariah saw that all eyes were pinned on her and waiting. "All right, here goes nothing."

They beheld her making snow angels for the first time. Mariah began to laugh and cry. J. J. jumped down to comfort her, but she put snow in his face and down his back then giggled. Everyone climbed off the wagon, and the snow wars were on. The evening slipped away, and everyone was exhausted, wet, and cold. The wagon pulled up in front of a brightly lit place. The electricity was on. The men smiled as they helped the children and Mariah down.

Standing at the door in aprons were Sara and Karen. Their wave was rewarding. Jud remembered that when he and Ken returned home to Ken's mother's house after camping out, there had been the sweet smell of treats.

"Jud, where did you go?"

"Hello, sweetheart. You've never looked lovelier than this moment." He picked her up and carefully spun her around. Slowly, he put her down. She kissed his cheek.

"What's brought all this on?"

The children chattered and scurried from their clothes.

Jud nodded as he tried placing a call to the airport and then to Tom. He turned and said, "Ken, Sara, thanks for sharing your home, friendship, and the holiday, but Karen, we need to pack. Our flight leaves at three in the morning. Dad will meet us at the airport."

J. J. hugged Jud and wished them a safe journey back home. Then he walked over to Mariah and nudged her shoulder. "Come on, honey. Let's get to Spencer's. Stay close, and we'll both stay warm. Thanks, Sara, for the blanket. See ya." He lifted Mariah on the tractor and slid in behind her. The night was lit with heavenly stars, and the moon sparkled in its fullness. She kissed his neck and settled back into him.

19

Karen was delighted to be on the plane headed home, and she was anticipating the warmth of her own bed. She sat back, closed her eyes, and thought, *Mariah and J. J.'s wedding was wonderful, and it was great to see everyone again, maybe even Eurlene. No, well, maybe not. But it was a nice surprise to stay with Sara and Ken.* She adjusted the seat and whispered, "There's no place like home."

Karen blinked her eyes and momentarily looked at the children who were fast asleep, and then she glanced over at Jud. He was relaxed and so handsome. She thought, *How changed is the man I cherished, or is it me who has changed?*

The plane hit an air pocket, and Jud reached his hand over to her. She placed her hand on his and noticed his long fingers. He folded his fingers over hers, and she brought them to her lips and kissed them.

Jud scooted down and rested his head on the back of the seat. She saw him drifting when a stewardess asked, "Sir, care for a pillow?"

He nodded. The woman fluffed the pillow and placed it behind his head. Karen watched as the woman lingered and drank in his good looks and ruggedness. Karen squeezed his hand and silently smiled for she knew he was most definitely hers. The green-eyed monster was killed. Maybe.

The children awakened and were herded from the plane. Rubbing their eyes, they saw Grandpa Tom. "Hi. Here we are."

"I see. Let's get the luggage, Jud."

Karen placed her arms around Luke and Luci. She turned and saw Jud's dimpled face welcoming his father. They hugged and slapped each other on the back. Tom said, "Karen, you're looking great. How far along are you now?"

Karen sighed. "Tom, people keep asking me. I need an appointment to see the doctor. He'll do an ultrasound. Perhaps I can get in by next week." In the same breath, she said, "How's Dora, and did anyone extra sign in at the bed-and-breakfast?"

Tom placed a hand on each child's head and answered Karen. "Dora is fine. A newlywed couple saw the highway sign and stopped at the bed-and-breakfast on a whim. She made her special truffles, and the couple raved. I was secretly glad they came, for I sure enjoy her treats. She's something else in the kitchen."

Karen saw the pride flow from Tom's face when he spoke of his wife. The resemblance between her husband and his father was awe-inspiring. Both were tall, muscular, and lean. Tom's hair was salted with silver, and his eyes were a deeper green; the shape appeared the same on Jud. Their voices were similar, and their God-fearing ways came across in both sound and actions.

Luke and Luci were only too glad to climb into bed. Jud pulled the shades, and Karen tucked them under their covers. She bid good night to Tom and Dora after giving them a hug. As she stepped on the stairs, Jud smiled and placed a hand on her lower back. "Darling, I'll walk with you."

She reached for his arm and leaned on it for strength. The king-size bed felt welcoming. Karen sank on the downy feathers. She patted the edge for Jud, but sleep was drifting in. His voice seemed muffled, but warmth stretched across the sheets.

"Good morning, Tom and Dora."

Karen stood scrambling eggs and had country-fried potatoes fired up. The serving table held bacon, sausage links, toast, butter and homemade red berry jam from Claudia. A pot of fresh coffee and a pitcher of freshly brewed iced tea were nearby.

The guests were huddled together at the table, and the twins were already heading to the swimming area. Jud had his shirtsleeves rolled up and was waiting on Tom to ride into the bank for business. Dora helped set the table and wore a striking apron. She handed Karen a cup of hot mint chocolate green tea.

Dora filled Karen in on the young couple's daily activities, which were planned, noting that only dinner would need to be served. Karen sighed at the thought of fixing dinner. Already, her feet were swelling and her stomach seemed to grow overnight. And there was the matter of Christmas gift exchanges.

The phone rang. "Hello, this is Karen Day. How may I help you?"

"Karen, this is Lola from your doctor's office. Dr. March would like you to check into the hospital for your examination this week. He will run the tests there."

"What day?"

"Friday. Let's say, seven in the morning."

"Lola, I've jotted the information down. I'll be there, and thanks for calling. Bye."

Luke and Luci finished swimming and were dripping wet. They waited on Karen to know what they were doing next. Dora ushered the twins upstairs to shower and dress. They met their mother back in the kitchen.

Dora fussed with the vegetables and motioned to Karen to sit.

"What are you fixing, Dora?"

She smiled. "Vegetable soup. The weather is cold enough, and with creamy grilled cheese sandwiches, it's fast and very delicious. I want you to rest. Karen, we can stay for another week or two. If you don't mind?"

"Oh yes, please stay. Jud will be happy if both of you can extend your stay. I know the twins will be thrilled." Karen waddled to the bathroom, shaking her head. "I forgot this part too. Frequent visits." She washed her hands.

Karen flopped on the couch with feet propped and couldn't believe what time it was when she woke up. She heard the dinner bell ring and saw Jud headed her way. He offered a hand and a gentle kiss. "I'm glad you were able to rest."

"Be right with you. Bathroom calling."

As Karen entered the kitchen, the phone rang. Jud took the call. Karen saw a raised vein appear in Jud's neck. His brows furrowed. He placed the receiver then dialed another number. This time he stood with his back to her and a hand in his pocket, jiggling coins.

Jud strolled over to Tom and whispered in his dad's ear. Tom jerked and sternly looked at Jud, shaking his head. The meal was served, and their conversation was sparse.

The guests were busily playing dominoes with Luke and Luci.

Jud bit into his second truffle and said, "Karen, I won't be able to take you to the doctor for your next couple of visits." He wiped his mouth and reached for another truffle then sipped hot black coffee.

"Why, Jud? I've already made the appointment." Karen pouted.

Tom placed a hand on Dora's shoulder and squeezed it. "Karen and Dora, Jud must catch a flight to New York. It seems Miss Phyler has had a fall. The hospital thinks she only has a nasty ankle sprained. But being that Jud knows her the best and she is without a family, he has been summoned there"—he smiled and looked at Dora—"and Karen, we are staying here."

"But Dora doesn't drive." Tears threatened, and one slipped down her cheek.

"Karen, honey, Dad will operate at the bank, and Dora will attend the bed-and-breakfast and help out with the twins. I'm sure you're not as helpless as you think." He kissed her cheek. "You can take a cab to the doctor, but not a bus. I'm sorry, Karen, but poor Miss Phyler and the NYC's bank…"

"I know Eurlene is away on a crisis, and I'm being selfish. I know she would take care of business if she could. I'm sorry, Jud, Tom and Dora. It's my mood swings. I don't know why I'm laughing."

Dora gave Karen a hug. "It's all right, dear. We'll get through this. Think of all the women of long ago having babies on the prairie." Dora tilted her head. "We'll be all right, promise."

The phone rang again and Karen jumped. Jud answered the phone. "Wait, I'll put you on speaker." He pushed a button and turned toward Karen. "You there?"

"Hello, Karen." The line crackled, but she knew the voices.

"Mother, Dad, how are you? Louise and Sam, are they enjoying the trip?"

"We are having so much fun. Wish you were here. What's the doctor had to say?"

"Mother, we were stranded in Mississippi with a snowstorm for over a week. But things are almost back to normal. Except for my mood swings. I have a doctor's appointment on Friday."

"Darling, things will work out. How are our grandchildren?"

"Just find. They're playing board games with our guests."

"Are they winning?"

She heard her father laugh then he came on the phone. "Karen, your mother and I will be delayed in coming home. We signed on with Sam and Louise for another sightseeing trip. We should be back in four to six weeks. Right before the baby is due."

Karen gasped. The lines sputtered, and Jud squeezed her hand and said, "See you then."

Tom patted Karen's head. "It's all right."

"Poor Sara." Karen struggled as she edged up from the chair and padded in to her guests while carrying some truffles.

Jud stopped at the doorway of the parlor and bade Karen and the twins farewell. "I'll call after I see Miss Phyler."

"What about our gift exchange? And where will you be staying?"

"I'll let you know when I'm settled. You and the kids open your gifts anytime. I packed mine." He kissed Karen and handed her a package, and then he walked out the door, turned, waved, and continued to the waiting cab.

Dora eased in and played games with the guests and twins. She scored high scores. Karen sat quietly by herself. She felt down, alone, and rejected somehow. An idea hit. She would call Sara.

"Hello. This is Sara."

"It's me, Karen. I just heard from Mother. They all seem to really be enjoying themselves."

Sara was giggling. "I'm sure they are, but you didn't call about them. I know you. What's going on?"

"Oh, woe is me is back." Karen let out a breath. "You know, clothes not fitting; it's hard to sit, stand, or walk; and our mother is gone. And now so is Jud."

"Are Tom and Dora still at your place?"

She sniffled. "Yes."

"Okay, so why is Jud not there?"

"Sara, Old Miss Phyler fell while in New York. The hospital called Jud to come to her aid."

"Karen, she doesn't have any family, and Jud is like a son to her. So what's really bothering you?"

"Well, he will be tending to Eurlene's bank."

"Karen, I don't believe you. That green-eyed-monster is still alive. Now, girl, let's pray."

Karen made one last plea. "Who's helping you out besides Ken?"

"Funny you asked." Sara moved a squeaking chair. "Do you have a minute?"

"Let me reach for a cup of hot tea and a snack. There, I've pulled the old faithful chair up to the phone. Go ahead. I'm listening."

A chuckle escaped. "Where to begin? Eurlene hired her architect Mr. Afee to finish Sam's place, but when he came, Eurlene had left with Spencer. He scared J. J. and Mariah when Mr. Afee hammered away. J. J. went to the kitchen with a baseball bat." Sara began laughing. "Both men were surprised, but thankfully, J. J. recognized him. Well, the newlyweds needed a place to stay for Mr. Afee could not reschedule the work. So Mariah and J. J. are staying here. Hang on."

Karen tapped her short nails while waiting.

"Karen?"

"I'm back. Duty called."

"Now, Ken received a call from the woman who lives in the artist cottage on Sam's, well, it's now Spencer's property. A cattle order came in, and the ranch manager couldn't get a hold of Sam or Spencer, so that's why Ken was called. Ken is helping in rounding up the wild herd."

"What?"

"Karen, all I could think of was Claudia. She would love this old Wild West adventure." They both chuckled.

"Yes, she would be hot on the trail."

Sara yawned. "It's hard to believe, but J. J. manned up and took on full responsibility of the bank while Ken is on the roundup. Oh, and come to find out, the New York City's architect is also a real cowboy. He has a farm down the way from Spencer's."

"Why didn't the town people help out? Did Ken even try to ask for help at the feedstore?"

"He did, but no one was available. If J. J. hadn't stopped by the house for Mariah's things, we wouldn't know Mr. Afee volunteered to help Ken. The men are camped out on the open range, and they have hundreds of acreage to cover. Ken will be gone for about four weeks."

"What? You're alone without help?"

"Karen, I have Matthew and Timmy and—"

"Who's left? Your mother and Sam are traveling, and I'm sure J. J. is head over heels at the banking business and with evening chores. Not to say with his own business and being a newlywed."

"Karen, you've forgotten about Mariah and Miechael." Sara laughed then said, "Mariah's a sight, wearing nine-inch heels and designer clothes but with an apron. You wouldn't believe it, but just let her loose in the kitchen, and she is a great chef."

"You could blow me over. Mariah?"

"Yes, when she was abroad she studied food preparation. Her skills are way up there. She's made pies, cookies, and bread. The house smells so good." Sara sighed. "However, the doctor placed me on semi bed rest. He said everything is fine, and the baby is doing well. I was having early prelabor pains. So he wants to wait as long as possible before our little Ruth Louise is born."

"Sara, sweet name. Does your mother know the name you picked out?"

"No, she doesn't. Karen, I have to hang up. The bathroom is calling. Take care and call me anytime. Love you, my friend."

The dial tone buzzed as Karen stared. She also trotted off to the bathroom and said good night to her bed-and-breakfast guests and to Dora. She met the twins upstairs, and they waited for Karen to read to them. She selected several books, and it was Luci's time to pick out which story. Luci's favorite Bible story was about handsome, rugged King David. Then Karen gave the twins their gifts. An hour later, she tucked the children in bed but was surprised when Luke took her hand and slowly walked her into her bedroom. "Sit, Mommy." His small hand patted the bed.

Karen all but flopped. Luke slipped off her slippers and rubbed her feet. He reached for his dad's pillow and placed it under his mother's legs. "Mommy, you rest. I'll take care of you while Dad's away."

Karen turned her head. The sentiment pierced straight to her heart. Clearing her throat, she said, "Can you fluff the pillow and pull the cover up? Thanks, Luke. Get the light, please." Her eyelids would not stay open. She heard the door shutting and Dora's soft voice.

When Friday came, it was gorgeous outside. The sun brightly shined and there was almost zero wind. The cabbie focused on helping Karen into the cab. She let herself down, and he shut the door.

Karen was experiencing some back twinges, but she really wasn't in any pain. She was happy that Dora's gift consisted of new items to wear. It seemed overnight that her clothes didn't fit.

The ride to the hospital seemed long, but it was nothing compared to that long ago bus ride. Karen caught herself giggling. She lowly stated, "What a hot day it was, my first pregnancy and that bumpy ride. And of course the adventure was with my friend, Sara. And the bus broke down. The wait, the heat, and the misery."

The cabbie looked over his shoulder. "We're here." He helped her onto the sidewalk and assisted Karen slowly in through the hospital's doors, where a nurse greeted her. Karen paid and waved the driver on. She took a deep breath, smiled, and squared her shoulders, saying, "Dr. March requested me to come in for some test. Where do I sign?"

"Karen, these are the forms, and if you have any questions, just ask. Turn the papers in when you are through. See, ring the bell."

Karen nodded and shuffled toward a seat. She felt a pain rush in her side and let out a gasp. Feeling embarrassed, she lifted her head and unfolded into a chair. She filled out the papers and scooted to the edge to find leverage to stand. She was stuck. Karen shifted in the chair and tried lifting her belly, but nothing worked. She began laughing uncontrollably, crying, and then finally, she peed her pants.

The nurse hurried to her side. "What's wrong? Has your water broken?"

Karen felt icky and was nervous. She started hiccupping. "No, but I'm stuck."

The nurse quickly summoned the custodian and someone else to remove the arm off the chair. She then ushered Karen, in a wheelchair, into the waiting room.

20

Karen rolled her blue eyes at the flat, narrow examining table with remembered cold metal stirrups and a way-too-small, thin cotton gown. The nurse said, "Strip down and tie the ties in front. The doctor will be right in."

Karen's mouth gaped. She wondered, *What doctor?*

"Hello, Mrs. Karen Day? I'm Dr. March's new assistant, Dr. Moonhart."

Karen thought, *He's so young.*

He folded his hands and added, "Dr. March is in the delivery room, and he asked me to run some basic tests. Let's first get you measured. Lie down, please, and scoot forward. A little more, you're doing a great job."

Karen saw a mask placed across his mouth as he slid on his gloves. She heard their snap. She breathed in and closed her eyes. The physical exam was so uncomfortable. The baby began kicking and went non-stop. She was sent to x-ray for a pictorial view. Five tubes of blood were drawn and her blood pressure was taken. They even checked her ears, nose, and throat. Nothing about oneself was private.

The former nurse came in the room. "Karen, we are moving you in to a private room for the night. Dr. March will see you in the morning. He said you just need to eat and rest."

Karen raised her head. "I wasn't expecting to stay tonight. Can I come back in the morning?"

The nurse patted her hand as she lifted the hand railing. "No." She smiled. Then she said, "You can call home after you're settled."

"Is there anything wrong with the baby?"

A smile traced the nurse's face as she wheeled Karen to her room. She hummed lowly. The nurse nodded to the orderly, and they helped Karen into bed. The nurse handed her the phone and said, "You may place your meal order. Menu is on the table. If you need anything just ring for the nurse, blue button." The older nurse backed out the door.

Karen hurriedly called home. On the second ring, Dora answered, "KD Bed-and-Breakfast."

"Dora, it's me, Karen."

"Anything wrong?"

"I don't think so, but Dr. March couldn't see me today, so he had his assistant run the tests. Dr. March insisted I stay the night and that he would talk with me in the morning when my tests are back."

"Well, the twins are fine. Tom will be here shortly and will offer his help with the guests. You just follow the doctor's orders. We'll see you tomorrow. Rest now. Bye."

Karen looked upward and said, "I should be feeling better, but I'm sad." She said, "I feel all alone. Be near."

A bubbly young girl brought in a meal. She helped Karen sit up and whizzed from the room. The phone rang. Karen jumped. She answered, "Hello?"

"Karen, are you all right? My father just called me."

"Jud, it's so nice hearing your voice. I'm fine. Dr. March was in with a delivery. So his new assistant ran my tests. Instead of coming back in the hospital tomorrow, the doctor had me spend the night."

"You sure, Karen?"

She quickly answered, "I should be home tomorrow."

"Did the doctor say how the baby is doing? Or when you are due?"

"No, he told me to rest. The baby seems fine because it's jumping." Karen giggled. "Jud, how are things at the bank, and how is Miss Phyler?"

"Miss Phyler is something else. She doesn't want to follow the doctor's orders. She's insisting she can handle the banking business. I had to threaten to fire her."

"Jud, you be sweet. She's probably scared. You know injury is new to her."

"I'll sweet her."

"Jud?"

"All right. I'll be gentle. About the banking business, people are rude and arrogant and very fast-paced. Although I've not personally had any trouble from anyone, it keeps me on my toes. I know for a fact that Eurlene is the best person suited for this branch. Or maybe Miss Phyler may be better." He chuckled and then said, "Karen, there is a lot of socializing one is expected to do here. I'm not that person anymore."

"Jud, you were born with a silver tongue, so don't even go there. It's you, I know. And I'm sure you will enjoy the arts and theater. I would if I were there."

"Karen, the bright lights are not in my interest any longer."

"Jud, I love you. Help Miss Phyler, do your penitence, and handle the bank."

"Sure, I'll attend the shows, dress the part, and even stop for having pictures taken between nursing Miss Phyler, but honestly I would rather be with you and our children. I love you, Karen, and I miss you. I'll call tomorrow? Sorry, Karen, I'm being paged."

The warmth from the call had ended, and only a buzz, buzz sound existed. Karen didn't understand her letdown feelings after the call; then tears began to fall. Just then volunteers came in holding magazines. "Here is a couple you might enjoy." They smiled and pushed the cart on down the hall.

Karen knew she must have dozed for she had a crick in her neck. She pushed a button, and the TV came on. It must have been around eleven in the evening for the news and weather was on. Karen found she was very thirsty, and she pushed the call button.

An unfamiliar nurse entered the room. "Good evening, Mrs. Day. I see you rested some. What do you need?"

"I would like some Jell-O and hot tea with a lump of sugar, please." Karen moved closer to the edge, and the nurse let down the side.

"Where are you going, Karen?"

"To the restroom." Karen let her gown flap for the ties wouldn't all meet.

The nurse said, "Wait." She slipped into and out of the room without being heard. On the chair, she laid a clean larger gown and a blanket with another pillow on top. At the side table sat the hot tea with toast, not Karen's requested Jell-O.

Karen washed up and changed gowns and placed the ties in the back. Out of habit, she pinched her cheeks. She fluffed the pillows and placed one behind her back for she noticed a dull ache. The baby became lively, and sleep wasn't happening. She looked at her swollen feet and puffy hands and big belly. She thought her face looked bloated. She recalled from before being told she glowed. She looked at herself, and there wasn't any glow, just rash-like patches appearing on her face.

It was three in the morning, and Karen's eye sockets hurt. She felt tender, as if she were a chicken plucked. An hour passed, and then finally, another nurse came in. "Karen, here's your breakfast, and look what came for you."

An overhead light appeared, and Karen blinked several times and adjusted her eyes. There sat a huge arrangement of flowers, a mixed grouping of yellow roses, purple sage, and white long-stemmed daisies. It was gorgeous and smelled heavenly. The flowers were from Jud. She held the card to her heart. *Even while busy, he had thought of me.*

The nurse popped in. "Are you finished with your food?"

Karen had forgotten about it and answered, "No, just leave the toast and coffee. The rest can go. Thanks."

Tom came through the doorway carrying a small case. He was smiling. "Dora had me to bring you this. There's makeup and a fresh change of lounge clothes. I didn't forget." He held up thick foam slippers.

Karen kissed his cheek and muttered, "Thank you."

His green eyes widened when he saw the flowers. Before he could say anything, Karen burst into laughter. "They're from Jud. Aren't they beautiful? He shouldn't have though."

Tom adjusted his silk tie, still smiling. "Has the doctor been in?"

Footsteps were heard; then, Dr. March appeared and said, ""Hello, Mr. Tom Day. Are you standing in for your son?"

Tom cleared his throat. "I am. How are things going with Karen and the baby? We all are dying to know if it's a boy or girl. Any thoughts on the matter, Doc?"

"Well, Karen and Tom, I can tell you—" But just then a page came.

"Paging Dr. March, paging Dr. March. You are wanted in OR." He nodded his head and said, "Sorry, I'll be back. Good to see you, Tom."

Karen watched as her doctor's coat jacket flapped with him out the door.

Tom's eyebrows were arched. "Karen, why don't you call Sara today and have a girl-to-girl talk session? I'll swing by later and see how things are going. Bye, darling."

She slumped down and turned off the light. She rolled to the right side and partly lay. Karen awoke to a jolt. She was in a sweat, and the baby was kicking. A nurse was taking her blood pressure and suggesting, "Karen, why don't you go and shower before the doctor comes?"

Feeling refreshed from the shower, she waddled and sat on an armless chair and dialed Sara. "Good morning."

"Karen, oh it's so nice to hear your voice. I was writing in my journal. So much has happened. But tell me, have you been to the doctor?"

"Funny, but I'm at the hospital." Karen's voice rose higher. "Don't be alarmed Sara, the doctor wanted to run tests and asked me to come in to the hospital for them. My doctor has been tied up with deliveries ever since. I've seen his new assistant, and he is way too young. Otherwise, I'm still waiting."

"Karen, isn't Jud with you?"

Sobbing, Karen answered, "No, he's not here. Remember, he's at Eurlene's bank, and he's taking care of Miss Phyler. His father and Dora are here. Tom's helping out at the bank, and Dora is helping with the kids and running the bed-and-breakfast."

"Karen, Karen, Karen. Your hormones are all over the place, and the green-eyed monster is rampant again. Think about the facts, Karen. You are getting excellent care and rest, something I don't get much of."

Karen interrupted. "Sara, Jud did send me flowers."

"Did you call and thank him? I'm sure he's a busy man and still he took time out for just you. Shame, friend, get over your self-pity."

Karen said, "No, I haven't called him. Sara, here comes Tom and Dora. Call me later. Oh Sara, when's the baby due?" The line was silent.

Karen wiped her eyes and pinched her cheeks. "Hey! Hi, you two."

Dora gave Karen a kiss. "Do you feel up to coming at the end waiting area? The children came to see you."

Tom was smiling. "Has the doctor been back?"

"Yes and no, but I've been poked and prodded and tossed about by nurses. I'm not at all a good patient." Karen shook her head while standing.

Tom voice was soothing.

"Karen, I'm sure this is not a picnic, but you only have another month or so—maybe." He offered his arm, and together, they slowly walked the hall's distance.

Luke stood. Luci stayed seated. Both twins in unison said, "Mother, it looks like they filled you with air."

Karen bit her bottom lip. "I've missed you, too." Karen kept standing and leaning more on Tom for there weren't any armless chairs, and she wasn't going to risk embarrassment again by being stuck.

Dora urged the twins to hug and kiss their mother. She looked at Karen and said, "Luke and Luci have missed your reading to them."

Luke, with arms partway around his mother's waist, said, "Grandma Dora got us a new animal book series. It's for third graders to read, but Mommy, we want you to read it to us." He pouted

Karen tucked him under his chin and said, "How about we take turns in reading?"

She tilted her head as Luci piped in, "Me too, Mommy."

Her back was aching from the pressure of standing. She placed her arms around them both, kissed their heads, saying, "I'll be home soon. Mind Grandpa Tom and Grandma Dora."

Tom nodded to his wife to leave with the children as he helped Karen to the room. The nurse was tapping her foot. "Mrs. Day, just look at you. Let's get you in bed and prop those legs!"

Tom reddened. He kissed Karen's cheek and waved from the doorway.

She lingered for a moment then toddled to the bathroom. "Okay, I'm ready to lie down."

"Karen, where do you hurt?"

"Where don't I hurt would be a better question. It's my legs, feet, and hands, and there are twinges in the back. Where is the doctor?"

"Not certain when he's due here. Lift your legs. There, does that feel better?" The nurse wiggled her finger. "I don't want you out of bed unless you get permission. This swelling has to be eased. Rest now." She closed the door as she left. Karen slept.

Bright and early the next morning, the overhead light shone. Karen rubbed and blinked her eyes, adjusting to the bright light. Dr. Moonhart was standing at the foot of her bed reading her chart. "Well, Doctor, are you discharging me?"

He looked down. "Karen, you're running a slight fever and are dehydrated. The nurse will hook an IV up for added protection. I conferred with Doctor March, and he is also concerned about your swelling and the water you're holding. I had Mr. Tom Day call, and everything is fine for your stay with us. He will be in later to bring you some more sleepwear. Hopefully, in a few days, everything will be fine and you'll be able to go home."

"What?"

"Don't talk, Karen, and keep this under your tongue." The nurse buzzed around hooking the filter lines into Karen. Her head was lowered and her feet raised and pillows were all around her. She tried moving her head, and the nurse said, "We've placed an ice collar around your neck. It's to help bring down the temperature. Rest."

"I'm hungry. I slept through lunch. Come on, I feel like a pin cushion."

The gray-haired nurse said, "Lift up."

What's this? Oh no, not a bedpan! Gees!" She rolled her eyes.

"Nurse, order Mrs. Day a soft meal and some orange juice."

"But I'm really hungry."

The doctor touched her shoulder. "If you're a clean plater, I will order you more Jell-O and maybe some toast served with a hot tea." He smiled and placed his pen in his coat pocket and left the room.

"Nurse, did my test come back? Am I having a boy or is it a girl? And do we have a better due date?"

The nurse scooted her glasses up. "Karen, Dr. March will be in. He left word that he wants to talk with you." She patted Karen's arm and added, "I put some water on your beautiful flowers. Did you see there is another arrangement? They are all white daisies."

Karen, shivering, muttered, "Who are they from?"

The nurse lifted the note. "Ah, they are from a Mr. Jud Day. Look, he's included a picture of an elder woman in a wheelchair. And here's one, it says, "taken of Jud." Wow, he's really a very handsome man." She padded back to Karen. "The card reads, 'I miss and love you Karen.' Look he drew a heart."

The nurse pulled the linen cover around Karen's shoulders and turned off the light. "Your meal will be in soon. The aide will let you know. Now rest."

Karen hadn't thought she was tired, but suddenly her lids felt heavy. Her mind began to drift. She could sense his nearness and the touch of his lips. Those green eyes like the sea and his chocolate wavy hair.

"Hello, Mrs. Day, your evening tray is here." The aide turned on the light and cranked up the bed and fluffed her pillows. She slid the tray over Karen's lap and waltzed out the door. Karen took a bite of Jell-O and saw mashed potatoes. No salt or butter. She flipped on the TV. It was fuzzy.

Karen glanced at the chair and saw that new nightwear had been delivered. She had missed Tom. Man, no adult conversation, nothing to watch on TV, and all this hook up. A cheerful nurse came in and asked, "Would you care for any assistance in bathing?"

"Yes, I would. It may make me feel better."

The tray was removed, and the makeup kit was set in its place. The nurse unplugged the lines and walked slowly with Karen to the shower. The nurse had her to sit down on a bench and let the water flow over her body. Karen was glad for the bubbly soap and squeezed the washrag over her neck and shoulders.

After drying with the huge fluffy towel, the nurse rubbed lotion on and helped placed the nightwear on Karen. Karen wrapped her arms around her shoulders and breathed in the freshness. After adding a touch of makeup, Karen was only too glad to get into bed.

The nurse said, "There, now you are all hooked back up. You won't need your ice collar the rest of the night." She handed Karen the magazines to read or thumb through. She paused and lowered the lights, saying, "Just touch the button when finished." The pillows were behind her head, and the nurse said, "Lights out in forty-five minutes with back position and legs elevated again. I'll be back."

Karen pushed the button, and the nurse station answered, "What do you need, Karen?"

"I would like some toast and hot tea if that's not too much trouble."

"Be right in."

Karen finished the last sip of tea, and the older nurse knocked and came in. "It's time to lie down, Karen." She shifted Karen easily into bed and adjusted the pillows and her position again. The nurse stroked Karen's face. "Pleasant dreams, dear." She whistled a soothing tune while lowering the bed and raising Karen's legs. She turned the light off and closed the door as she left.

Karen lingered as sleep evaded her. Her mind kept wandering on things to do.

21

Tom entered Karen's room. "Hello. How's the patient?" He smiled and said, "Dr. March called the B and B early this morning and asked me to be present since Jud is out of town." He kissed Karen's cheek and said, "I'm sorry. My son is out of town."

Karen was a little surprised, but she answered, "I know. And I think I'm good. My hands and feet are back to seminormal instead of looking like blown-up balloons."

The doctor stepped in, and Tom speed dialed Jud. "Hello, son, I'm in the room with Karen and Doctor March." Tom pushed on the speaker button.

"Hello, Mr. Day, glad you could join us by phone." The doctor turned and approached Karen. "Here's the good news. Karen, all your tests have come back excellent. Although, you gave us quit a scare because you needed to take in more liquid. Now I'm not able to give you the sex of the child, but Jud, Karen, and Tom, there are going to be twins again. Jud, drink your orange juice."

Jud was chuckling. "Already did so this morning, Doctor March. I remembered."

"Now, Karen, I'm releasing you, but you're on semi bed rest. No lifting and changing beds and etc. Tom confirmed he and Dora are staying and will care for you."

"Thanks, Dad, call me later. Miss Phyler is on my other line. Love you, Dad. Bye, Dr. March."

The doctor continued, "Now Karen, you must drink lots of liquids. And bed rest is a must, at least three times a day." He jotted on the charts, adding, "The twins are due within three, maybe four weeks. It's a little sooner than expected. However, the longer they stay inside, the better. If you keep having pains, don't hesitate to call me or come straight to the hospital. Karen, are you all right?"

Karen was smiling and rubbing her stomach and could only nod.

The doctor scribbled orders and signed Karen's release papers. He shoved them into Tom's hand as he was being paged to emergency for another delivery.

Tom scooted from room to room to sign Karen out. Karen waited for the nurse and wheelchair. She was going home, and her stomach growled.

She entered the house where the phone rang. She answered, "Hello."

Sara replied, "Hi, friend, I found the hospital had sent you home. I guess everything is good? Well I have some news for you."

"What? Tell me then I'll tell you mine."

"Can you believe that Mariah drove me to the doctor?" Excitedly, she added, "Everything checked out great. Our Ruthie Louise is due in three to four weeks instead of two months out. Wow, she'll be here in no time. I just had to let you know."

"What is it Sara? I hear hesitation."

"Well, it would be nice to tell Ken, but who knows when he'll be home from the cattle drive?"

"Sara News, you know he would want to know the information about your little precious as much as you did. What do the boys think?"

"Matthew is happy, because he's not going to be the baby anymore. And Timmy pats my belly and talks to his sister a lot." Sara started laughing.

"The doctor said I'm healthy as a horse. Of course it's the country living. You've got to love it." Sara continued to laugh. "Tell me what your doctor said. Is it a boy or a girl?"

"Friend, sit."

" Well, what?"

"We're having twins again, and I'm due about the same time you are."

Sara was really laughing. "Get out of here, Karen. Really twins? Wow. Do you know their sex?"

Karen was laughing also. "No, that will have to wait, but not for long either. Can you believe we're due at about the same time? I wish you were here. It's sad our mothers won't be home when we deliver. But, Sara, we have each other, and I want to share my devotional verse with you. It's found in Hebrews 13:5b. It reads, "I will never leave thee, nor forsake thee. So see, we have the promise from Jesus. He's with us always. We can call on Him."

"Karen, thanks. I needed that." Sara cleared her throat. "Is Dora doing the dinners and all else?"

"Yes, she is, and she is so loving. I'm glad we are having this time together. By the way, Dora called Joan, Jud's mother, to let her know about the coming twins and my bed rest. Joan sent her regards and a basket of fruit." Karen yawned. "Sorry."

"Where is Jud's mother?"

"Joan and Eli were at an airport, headed on another of their world travels. They'll keep in touch. Before Joan hung up, she said, 'Best wishes. And then she blurted out, "I hoped this will be Karen's last pregnancy.' She spoke about my age, the responsibilities, and the cost of living. I know she's right about most, but she rubs me the wrong way."

Sara interrupted, "Karen, Karen."

She let out a sigh, saying, "I know, she's an egg. But you girl must keep trying to work things out with her. Look at how you and Jud communicate. It is through love, and God, which changed him."

"You're right as usual, friend. Oh, I felt a twinge. Sara, I need to lie down, and you should rest also. Tell Mariah, J. J., and the kids I said hello and be good. Thanks for calling and for the pep talk. Bye."

Sara was humming when J. J. entered the kitchen. He poured himself a cup of coffee and placed the creamer back in the refrigerator, letting the door slam. Mariah pointed her index finger at him and backed him into a seat.

"What?"

"Don't what me." Mariah's lip trembled. "My cake needs to sit and cool. The directions indicated no noise." Mariah stomped her foot. "I know the cake is flat now, and Sara showed me how to make it. It's taken hours." Mariah hunched forward and cried.

J. J. went to Mariah's side, but she moved away. She banged and slammed pots and pans everywhere. She dropped the flour, and it splattered. Matthew began patty cake in the flour, and soon Timmy and Miechael, thinking it was a group play, got on the floor and spread the flour more.

Sara's mouth gaped. J. J. had his hands up in the air. "Now what? Come on, Mariah."

Sara tried to offer her help, but Mariah ran from the room, and only the sobs and the clicking of her nine-inch heels were heard. J. J. threw the towel and slammed the door again, heading for the barn.

Sara threw up her hands and asked the children to come by her side. She took Timmy's hand and reached for Matthew's and nodded to Miechael to join in. Sara closed her eyes and gave a little squeeze to the children's hands. She spoke quietly. "Almighty One, hear my plea. Help Timmy, Matthew, and Miechael clean up the floor and carefully shake their clothes off outside and then guide them as they mop the floor from their fun. I thank You in advance, Sara." She opened one eye and saw the three boys sliding out from their clothes down to their briefs. Miechael got a basket and handed Timmy the clothes and asked, "Will you please shake these outside for Aunt Sara?"

Timmy began singing a song, "Jesus Loves Me." Miechael joined him, and so did Matthew. Soon the sweeping and mopping was done. Timmy said, "How does the floor look, Mommy?"

She smiled and said, "You three did a fine job. Now let it dry. I'm so proud of you, and I know Jesus is. How about getting your showers? And boys, please help Matthew."

"Ah, Mom, I'm a big boy."

"I know you are, Matthew, but help is good." She touched Miechael's cheek, asking, "Will you read to my boys, love?"

J. J. entered the room. His shoulders were slumped, and his red unkempt hair flew. His head was held low. "Sara, I let pride get in my way. I've failed you. I'm sorry. Are you all right?" He glanced around.

Sara cleared her throat and struggled to stand. "Come closer and take my hand. Has Mariah returned?"

J. J. hunched his shoulders and answered, "I think so. I thought I heard her upstairs talking with the kids."

"Wait here a moment."

"Mariah, you up there?" Sara yelled, still holding J. J.'s arm. She waddled to the phone.

"Coming, Sara. Miechael has finished reading, and I tucked the boys in bed."

With a hand on the phone Sara turned and faced J. J. "Think you could find Ken and give him a message? It may take you a couple of days in the backwoods, and it's dangerous."

Mariah stomped her foot and pouted. "Why does J. J. need to find Ken, Sara?"

"Well, missy, after I call your mother and leave her a message, you are taking me to the hospital. Ruthie Louise is not going to wait for anybody." Sara locked eyes with Mariah. "And I am going to have this one in the hospital!"

Mariah walked over to J. J. and hugged him. In her sweetest voice, she said, "You'll be really careful, won't you?"

He grinned and held her for a moment. "My middle name is Adventure. Yeah, I'll be careful." He kissed Mariah, lingered, and then said, "I'm sorry about your cake. I'm sure it's good. Would you pack me a brown bag for the taking?"

"I will."

"Sara, what do you want me to say to Ken when I find him?"

"J. J., let him know the baby decided to come early, and all is good." Sara giggled. "With this being a weekend, there's no need to worry about the bank. Just put the closed sign up for good measure." Sara patted her stomach. "Ruthie, the smart one."

Mariah left to help J. J. pack. "Thanks, but I need only what I have on, for there's nowhere to change." He reached and tied on the handkerchief. Their hands touched. Mariah shivered, and J. J. bent and kissed a willing and leaning-in Mariah.

"Hey, you two," Sara said. "The boys should be fine for a few hours tonight while you drive me to the hospital, Mariah, but I expect you to come straight back to the house and take care of them, and you will need to help them with chores. All right? You might want to change into grubby clothes and tie shoes, maybe boots, while helping."

The look on Mariah's face said everything, but she stammered, "I will take care of the boys and help. Sara, I promise."

Sara leaned forward with a pain. "Whew. Mariah, get the truck or something! My bag is sitting by the closet. Bye, J. J. Hurry."

The phone rang. Sara was puffing. "Hello?"

"Sara, did you call?" But not stopping, Sylvia continued, "The answering machine must have been full for it recoiled with a voice like yours and one like my mother's."

"I did call Sylvia. I want you to know that Mariah has been helping me out. And Ken is on a roundup while J. J. has operated the banking business. However, J. J. is on his way to find Ken. Ruthie Louise is about to be born. I wanted you to pray for this delivery and for our household." Sara began puffing again. "Bye, Sylvia. Don't worry, just pray."

"Ready, Sara? I'm scared."

"Mariah, take my hand and help me into the car. Don't fret. Just drive. A little faster would be good."

With a screech, Mariah pulled up in front of the hospital. She quickly opened Sara's door and walked her through the emergency doors. Sara was bending and puffing and holding her side. "Get me a wheelchair!"

A nurse passing by noticed the commotion and hurriedly attended to Sara. "I've got it from here, miss. Thanks."

Mariah pinched her lips. She had been dismissed, but she knew Sara needed her at the house to care for the boys. She squared her shoulders and gunned the motor. The Bentley whizzed down the road.

What a sight. Mariah had on Ken's hip boots and J. J.'s outdoor jacket. Through rummaging around the shed, she found leftover breathing masks. Timmy held his sides when Mariah stepped into the barn.

Mariah took the pitchfork and started slinging.

Miechael started chuckling, but he quickly gathered the straw and spread it all around after his mother cleaned the stall. Timmy, still laughing, got the oats and began feeding the horses. Matthew gathered the brown chicken eggs. They worked, it seemed, for hours, and Mariah was a mucky mess. She said, "I'm glad my fans can't see me now. And they call this living. Work all day just to do it all over the next day. To cook and cook and cook some more." She leaned on the rake and dwelled a little longer. "No, they can keep this country living. I'll take the city anytime," she mumbled. She stared at the horizon wondering when Eurlene and Spencer would get back and hoping Eurlene and Spencer could cope with the children. What a terrible thing—children losing both mother and father.

Matthew tugged on her arm. He said, "Miss Mariah, will you play with me? Where's my Mommy?"

She panicked. What was she to say? Mariah yawned to cover up no answer. She tapped him on the shoulder. "Let's put the eggs away, change, and then play tag. Come on, boys."

The phone was ringing off the hook. Breathlessly, Mariah answered. "Hello, this is Mariah Brown." She recognized the voice.

"Mariah, is Sara around?"

"No, Karen. I took her to the hospital late last night. I haven't heard anything, though. It's just the boys and me here right now. Can I help?"

"No, but thanks. I just wanted to let her know the doctor has ordered me back into the hospital for the cramping has become intense, and my back is really aching. I'm waiting on Tom to take me. When she calls, let her know, okay? Oh, Tom's here. Bye."

Mariah stood looking at the silent phone. She heard the shower, but she couldn't move, and just said, "What a hot mess. Tom instead of Jud is with Karen. Dora is watching the twins, and Ken is out helping rustle cattle, and J. J. out riding the range. And I am stuck here in the wilderness." She hung up the receiver and continued. "Both Sara's and Karen's mothers are away, and my mother seems so far and Grand Ma Mere, heaven only knows where she is." Mariah walked to the back door and looked into the heavens. Unwanted tears slid down her face. *All right, You have my full attention. The men are all helping someone else somewhere away from their homes and families. You have placed Dora and me in new adventures, and yet the knowledge of the Almighty we need and want, as our march of life continues on.*

Mariah felt a warm hand slide around her waist. As she looked, she saw a now young, independent, strong, and wise preteen son. His smile deepened as he hugged his mother. "We'll be fine. Uncle Ken told me when I felt overwhelmed to look at God's creation." Miechael spread his hands upwards. "See the many numerous stars, Mother? God named them. Uncle Ken said God promises never to leave us nor forsake us. Isn't that grand?" His dark, dark eyes searched his mother's then he said, "Do you know this God as your Savior? Let's get some hot chocolate, and let me show you how."

Mariah could only follow him. As he served his mother and urged her to take a sip, he set his cup down and opened the huge family Bible. "See Mother, Romans 3:23 reads: 'For all have sin and come short of the Glory of God.' Mother, put your name where it says 'all.' Look here, Romans 6:23 reads: 'For the wages of sin is death, but the gift of God is eternal life.' Miechael flipped through the pages and showed Mariah where God said in John 14:6, 'Jesus saith unto him, I am the way the truth and the life: no man cometh unto the Father, but by me.' Then he turned to John 3:16–17 and read: *'For God so loved the world that He gave his only begotten Son; that whosoever believeth in Him should not perish, but have everlasting life. For God sent not his Son into the world to condemn the world, but that the world through Him might be saved.*

Miechael scooted his chair closer to his mother and made eye contact, saying, "This is what Jack showed me. Don't you see, Mother? We each need Him personally, and no one can accept Him for you but yourself."

Matthew and Timmy had slipped in to the room and had gathered around. They were listening to Miechael's readings and explanations. Timmy raised a little hand. Miechael turned to his cousin. "What is it, Timmy?"

"I want to know this Jesus."

Miechael's smile widened, "Let's join hands. Mother, you pray and then Timmy you pray, confess your sins, and ask Him in."

Suddenly, Mariah didn't feel alone. She breathed easier and had an unknown enlightenment and happiness she had never obtained. She didn't know how, but for the first time she knew that for her husband, J .J., Ken, Sara, Louise, Sam, Kate, Donald, Sylvia, Jon, the Ma Meres, Tom, Dora, Joan, Eli, Eurlene, Spencer, their new family, Jud, Karen, even Miss Phyler, and of course Claudia and Jack, would all work out, for she had relinquished herself and now she knew the One who was in control. She sang.

Karen Day's Recipe: Mint Chocolate Green Tea

Use six to eight regular size green tea bags.
Add one quart cold water to one gallon pan and bring to boil.
After boil, remove from heat and steep for fifteen minutes.
Wash and add three freshly cut chocolate mint leaves.
Cover pan.
In gallon container, put four cups of hot water.
Add in two cups sugar or substitute sweetener or honey (optional), to taste.
Squeeze tea bags in pan and slowly pour tea into container.
Add chocolate mint leafs (optional) from pan into container.
Cap container and shake or uncap and stir, but only with a wooden spoon.
Continue to fill container a fourth way from top and add ice.
Place in refrigerator overnight.
Enjoy!

www.ingramcontent.com/pod-product-compliance
Lightning Source LLC
Chambersburg PA
CBHW051651260626
47170CB00004B/1445